"Se

he insinuated softly

It seemed like an eternity before Brad let her go.

"Don't you ever kiss me again!" Sheena managed to get out, rubbing her hand over her mouth, which still stung from his punishment.

Somewhere along the way she had touched a raw spot. Because she hadn't appreciated his manliness? He had obviously expected her to weakly acknowledge his mastery.

"You can save that kind of demonstration for those who appreciate it. You're wasting your time with me," she continued.

"In that case we'll try again, and see if I can get it right." And his arms reached out for her once more.

Jane Corrie was born in County Kent in southwest England. Her first job as junior reporter on a local paper may have piqued her interest in writing, but it was only after her life took several twists and turns—two relocations to advance her husband's career and various jobs in the veterinary, dental and medical fields for Jane—that she finally gave in to her yearning to write. She took temporary work in order to set aside time to concentrate on her craft, and her efforts paid off. Her first book was published in 1974, with many more to follow. Jane now lives in northern England. She enjoys painting in oils, although writing romances remains her greatest love.

Books by Jane Corrie

Don't miss any of our special offers. Write to us at the following address for information on our newest releases.

Harlequin Reader Service
901 Fuhrmann Blvd., P.O. Box 1397, Buffalo, NY 14240
Canadian address: P.O. Box 603,
Fort Erie, Ont. L2A 5X3

Muldoon Territory

Jane Corrie

Harlequin Books

TORONTO • NEW YORK • LONDON
AMSTERDAM • PARIS • SYDNEY • HAMBURG
STOCKHOLM • ATHENS • TOKYO • MILAN

Original hardcover edition published in 1988
by Mills & Boon Limited

ISBN 0-373-17039-4

Harlequin Romance first edition June 1989

CHAPTER ONE

SHEENA MULDOON FAIRBURN took note of the discreet but very august gold letting on the side of the Land Rover that had arrived to pick her up at Canberra's main coach station.

She was tired, and in need of refreshment, not only in the food line, but in the wish for a cool shower to wipe away the inevitable stains of travel, so her impulse was one of intense irritation when her eyes landed on the gold lettering that declared positively that this vehicle was the property of the Muldoon clan.

The name had haunted her from early childhood, and although her name as registered by her proud mother on her birth certificate was indeed Muldoon Fairburn, Sheena knew it was only her pride that had made her mother declare the connection. Her mother had had a right to the name, she had been born a Muldoon, but had since married John Fairburn, and that, Sheena had reasoned, should have removed the name of Muldoon from the records, but her mother had thought otherwise, obstinately hanging on to the name although the Victoria Muldoons had long since gone their separate ways from the Canberra Muldoons.

The only surviving connection had been through her great-grandmother, who was apparently as stubborn as Sheena's mother was in preserving some link between the families, a link that had been unceremoniously cut off when the second son of the thriving Muldoon family dairy estates had been bitten by the gold fever and joined the rush to Victoria.

As the Canberra Muldoons had gone from strength to strength, the Victoria Muldoons had slipped into the backwater of social prominence. Sheena had been brought up on the history, and on her mother's demise, ten years after her husband's, she had been dismayed to find that her sister, Mary, fully intended to carry on with the bowing and scraping attitude towards the Canberra branch.

It wasn't until she was at the student nursing college that Sheena was able fully to understand this slavish devotion to what, to her, was just snobbery, but Mary had kept certain things to herself, as her mother must have done through those lean years of making ends meet after the death of their father.

Mary had been just eighteen when their mother had died, and had been left to look after Sheena at fourteen, and Shaun their brother, twelve.

It had never occurred to Sheena that there had been a guiding hand behind their upbringing, particularly in the material sense. The summons from her great-grandmother, who had written suggesting that Sheena spend a few months with her, as she put it, to help liven up a lonely existence, made Sheena see red. 'We've managed without them for all these years,' she replied angrily when Mary showed her the letter. 'She's rich enough to get paid help, isn't she? I've got my Finals coming up in six months time, and I'm not wasting all that swotting just to curry favour with those snobs!'

Mary's quiet answer had rocked the floor under Sheena's feet. 'We owe Great-Grandmother a lot,' she said. 'Who do you think helped us out after father died? And helped pay for my wedding? Not to mention allowing you to take up a nursing career, and pay for Shaun's school books and clothes?'

Sheena had just stared at Mary, bereft of speech, then she swallowed. 'But . . . but I thought your salary paid for all those things. You always said I hadn't to worry, that you had enough, that your salary was good——'

Mary smiled. 'I suppose that was Mother's fault. I agree she ought to have told us when we were older, but it was awkward for her. You see, the money came by Banker's Order each month, and although Mother knew where it came from, she couldn't acknowledge the payment because she knew that our grandfather would have been furious if he had found out that she was sending us money. She told Mother this years ago, so although Mother had her pride, we needed the money, and for Gran's sake she accepted the terms.'

Charity wasn't always taken gracefully, and Sheena learnt that fact the hard way. She knew deep down that she ought to be very grateful, and she would have been, had she been told the fact long ago. It wasn't as if a complete stranger had suddenly issued them a blank cheque. Great-Grandmother was kin, even though she was still a stranger to Sheena.

All these thoughts went through Sheena's mind on the journey to Canberra, trying to work up some enthusiasm for the task in hand. She wanted to be a nurse, and here she was on her way to be a companion to her great-grandmother. Her great-grandfather had died six months ago, and it was shortly after this that the old lady had written to Mary asking for Sheena to visit her.

Sheena had read the letter, but could still not determine what her great-grandmother had in mind for her. It all depended, she thought sardonically, on how they got on together. On how pliant she would find Sheena. On this thought, she gave a deep sigh. It was not in her nature to bow and scrape, no matter how much she owed her relative. Having inherited her father's proud nature and lamentably short temper, it would, she thought, be simply a matter of time before they fell out.

She had it in mind to ask the driver of the Land Rover to give her fifteen minutes or so in which to freshen up before she was taken to meet her great-grandmother, but one look at the cold, expressionless face of the man as he stepped out of the vehicle and stared around in search of his passenger drove all such thoughts out of her mind.

Now he spotted her, and walked with swift but sure strides towards her. Sheena thought she detected a certain tightening of his lips as he approached her. 'Miss Fairburn?' he asked in a deep voice, as intimidating as his features.

Sheena particularly noted the way the Muldoon bit was left out of the name, but as she preferred to be know as Miss Fairburn she had no quarrel with this omission, only with the method of approach.

She nodded, and picked up her small suitcase, leaving the larger one for the man to carry.

Sheena could not be sure, but she sensed a certain disdain in his attitude as he picked up her large, shabby suitcase, and it was all she could do not to order him to leave everything to her, that she would get a taxi to take her the rest of the way.

After stowing her luggage in the back of the vehicle, he indicated that she should occupy the passenger seat in the front, and Sheena felt that she was being honoured by not being shoved at the back along with the luggage.

By now, she had developed a healthy dislike towards the man, whoever he was, and she fervently hoped that the rest of the staff were more approachable or her visit would be shorter than either she or her great-grandmother had envisaged.

'Brad Muldoon's the name,' the man said abruptly, as he got in beside her and started up the engine.

Sheena blinked at this rather unorthodox introduction, but felt a spurt of surprise. Her green eyes widened as she took stock of her companion, trying to fit him in to what little she remembered of the family. Pure Irish stock, she recalled, as indeed this man was, with his rugged features and black hair. At that moment his eyes met hers, an incredible bright blue, and about as warm as a mountain range.

Unabashed, Sheena went on with her observation. Tall, maybe six feet, and broad with it, very self-assured. Lingering on his lightweight fawn jacket and trousers, down to his hand-made shoes, she wondered how she could have mistaken him for a servant. Tiredness, she thought, as she closed her eyes, and murmured, 'Cousin.'

'Extremely distant,' he replied, in a tone of voice that suggested that even that wasn't distance enough. Sheena came out of her fitful doze with a fresh temper. What an obnoxious man he was!

'Of course,' he went on in a drawl, 'it depends on how you look at it. We're proud of our name, and our ancestors, but Gran's prouder than is good for her. Any idea why you've been sent for? he asked abruptly.

Sheena had been looking at the tall buildings that seemed to stamp authority on the surrounding landscape. She had tried hard to ignore the wretched man. Now she was forced to reply. 'Only that Great-Grandmother felt in need of some companionship,' she said.

She felt the man stare hard at her as if in disbelief. Then he gave a offhand shrug. 'In that case, I'd better put you wise,' he said. 'Gran's hatched up a plot. I suspect she's been nurturing it for years. I'm expected to fall overboard for you, and complete the family circle.'

Sheena swallowed, then blinked, and turned towards him. He didn't believe in pulling his punches, did he? She noticed the sardonic twist of his lips as he studied her reaction, while she struggled for words.

'So you didn't know,' Brad drawled. 'I did wonder.'

Sheena's first thought was to ask to be taken back to the coach station, if only to prove to this detestable man that he need have no worry where she was concerned. He could go back to his grandmother with a clear conscience, say she hadn't been on the coach, and·Sheena would think up some excuse as to why she hadn't been able to visit. A sudden illness, anything would serve. Even Mary wouldn't expect her to hang around after receiving such a mind-boggling proposition from such a man as this.

Her second thought was to be as obnoxious as the man was, and give him a taste of his own medicine. 'How nice,' she said, forcing a note of lightness into her voice. 'You've no idea how depressing being poor can be.'

She heard the swift intake of breath, and felt a surge of satisfaction that she had got through that self-satisfied demeanour of his.

'I'm sorry to disillusion you,' he replied through stiff lips,' but no change in your financial condition will be coming from the Muldoon estates. I would have thought your family had done well enough through the years by Gran's contributions. Don't you think you've scrounged enough?'

Sheena wished he hadn't been driving. It wasn't safe to hit a man in charge of a vehicle, but her fingers itched to deliver a blow. The worst of it was, he was right, but it wasn't her fault that her mother had agreed to accept financial help for all those years. 'My mother was a Muldoon,' she said quietly. 'You seem to forget that. I don't know what branch you hail from, but whatever side it was, it appears they were singularly lacking in family feeling.'

'So that's your view of things, is it?' he asked harshly. 'Well, I'll give you mine. We've worked hard for what we've got, through three generations, and we've carried your family for years. You're a Fairburn, not a Muldoon, and it's about time you started standing on your own feet.'

Sheena could have told him that was precisely how she saw things, but she was in no mood to agree with anything this man said. If he had told her the grass was green, she would have argued that it was purple. 'It was Great-Grandmother's money,' she flashed back at him.

'It was Muldoon money,' he grated out,' and if I have any say in the matter, there'll be no more payouts from this end.'

There certainly wouldn't, Sheena thought furiously. As soon as she was able, she would put Mary in the picture, and the money would be returned to sender. Between them they would manage to pay for Shaun's future requirements. She could take up an evening job in one of the cafés to keep them going when she took up her studies again.

'I think it would be a good idea if you were to turn round and take me back to the coach station,' Sheena said coldly.

'Suddenly lost all your family feeling, have you?' he asked sarcastically. 'Nothing in it, now that you know the score? And what about Gran? Doesn't she deserve some consideration for all that she's done for you? Or does the thought of fetching and carrying for an old lady sound a bit like hard work to you, especially as there'll be no pot of gold at the end of the track? No, we're not going back. The way I see it, you owe the

Muldoons, and this is one way you can show your gratitude for past favours.'

Sheena knew when she was beaten, but he wasn't having things all his own way. 'Aren't you worried that I'll worm myself into Great-Grandmother's favour?' she asked, with a glint in her green eyes that spelt trouble for anyone who knew her well.

'You won't do that by calling her Great-Grandmother,' he said grimly. 'You'll be told to address her as "Gran" as we all do, and no, I'm not worried about that. She can get as fond of you as she wants, but the estates are tied up. This mad scheme of hers to tie you in to the family was the only way she could ensure what she considers to be a settled future for all of you, but I'm afraid it's all pie in the sky. No amount of day-dreaming on her part is going to change the way things are. I don't advise you to encourage her, either; she knows how I feel. She knows me better than to hope I'll change my views on the matter.'

Sheena kept her glance on the passing landscape. Quite a speech-maker, wasn't he? She thought angrily. The Canberra Muldoons came from farming stock orginally, and she had a vague idea that they still ran farms, but this man was no farmer. City-bred and indoctrinated, she surmised, and if she had to take a guess at his occupation, she would have plumped for an accountant, which would account for his preoccupation with money.

The silence lengthened between them, and Sheena had to bite her lip to stop herself from shouting out that he had nothing to worry about where she was concerned. She had had one brush in the romantic stakes that had left her somewhat soured where the opposite sex was concerned. However much in love she had imagined herself to be with the young houseman at the hospital, she had soon been brought to her senses when he had decided that a consultant's daughter was a better bet for future promotion. Here was this pumped-up, conceited male actually telling her that she wasn't good enough to fill the role her great-grandmother had cast her in. It was bad enough to be turned down by Dr Bedson, but even worse to suffer the same fate from someone she didn't know, and certainly didn't like and never would like. The car swept up a long tree-lined avenue and turned off down a long driveway, but Sheena, oblivious of her surroundings, could only breathe in a sigh of relief that the journey was over, and she would soon lose this obnoxious man's company.

It was as well for Sheena's peace of mind that she was unaware, as the Land Rover drew up before a large modern ranch-type dwelling that even this relief was going to be denied her.

Sheena was surprised that her great-grandmother should choose to live in such a large, rambling dwelling. She had imagined her settled in one of the luxury flatlets that catered for the rich during their retirement years, and to find her living in what Sheena could only describe as a château in at least an acre of ground was a sharp reminder of the vast difference between the families' fortunes.

She found herself wondering what would have happened if her ancestor Benjamin Muldoon, had found the gold he sought when he deserted his family all those years ago. She sighed inwardly as she came out of her reverie to find her small case being thrust at her by the now impatient man, who was holding her larger case in his other hand. He was obviously in a hurry to relieve himself of both the case and his passenger.

This was one sentiment that Sheena was in accord with, and she followed his tall back towards the door of the building.

The moment Sheena entered the spacious hall, with its cool tiled flooring, hanging plants spilling down from the ceiling giving the impression that it was a conservatory, she was reminded of some pictures she had seen in a magazine of expensive residential properties in Spain. She vaguely wondered if this was where the idea came from. There was light everywhere. The sun streamed through huge plate-glass windows at each side of the entrance, and shone through a slightly tinted glass doorway. Sheena's companion strode on with confident steps.

This alone should have alerted Sheena to certain possibilities, but she was too intent on her surroundings and the coming meeting with her great-grandmother to allow room for any other consideration.

Eventually, after passing several doors, her companion strode into a sun-filled room and, after checking that Sheena was still with him, stood aside and let her advance into the room.

'Well, here she is, Gran,' he said, in his deep, well-modulated voice, as if, Sheena thought sourly, he had spent the morning looking for her, and having found her, had deposited her like a piece of missing luggage!

Her green eyes were still shooting sparks as they

met the cool, faded blue ones of her great-grandmother, who patted the empty seat beside her, indicating that Sheena should sit there.

As Sheena obeyed the silent summons, she could feel the man's eyes boring into her back. She walked towards the sofa where the old lady sat, and knew a sense of relief when she heard him say that he had work to do, and no doubt they would prefer to be alone.

'You mustn't mind Brad,' Great-Grandmother said, in a soft, almost soothing voice. 'His bark's worse than his bite, I can assure you,' she added with a smile. Her eyes roamed over the soft contours of Sheena's face, as if memorising them. 'You've got the Muldoon eyes, I see,' she said, 'and the looks. As pretty as a picture,' she summed up contentedly.

Sheena had been doing her own inventory, and liked what she saw, a frail old lady, her white hair swept back in a bun. Sheena knew that she must have been well past her eightieth birthday, but there was still strength of purpose in those faded blue eyes. But there were, however much she liked the old lady, a few things she ought to get straight right from the start of their acquaintance. 'I'm a Fairburn, Grandmother,' she said quietly, 'not a Muldoon.'

'Pooh,' said the old lady, waving a thinly veined hand at Sheena. 'Of course you're a Muldoon. I'm going to show you some photographs. You're a Fairburn, too, of course. A fine family.' She nodded at Sheena's quick stare. 'Oh, I've done some checking on that line, you may be sure. Good old farming stock, came from Queensland originally, drought nearly wiped them out to start with, and the

willy-willies finished them off in the end.' She gave
Sheena a bird-like glance with her head on one side.
'Hard life, girl, in those days. Not much better now,
but at least they've piped water to help them out
when it gets bad again. Too late for your Dad's
family, though.'

There was a short silence at this point, when it
seemed to Sheena that her great-grandmother went
into a reverie on the past, then she suddenly said,
'That's what Brad's hankering after. Wants to get
back to the land. I don't say he won't make a go of
it. He will. There's nothing that boy can't do if he
sets his mind to it, but he's head of the family now,
and there's other considerations to take into account
besides a pretty flibbertigibbet who would faint at
the sight of a cow calving!'

Sheena was at a loss to know just how to reply to
this rather rambling discourse, and wondered if the
old lady was liable to go off into such effusions
without warning.

She had gathered, with no little relief, that Brad,
who had collected her from the station, had a
prospective bride. She had no quarrel with this. In
fact, it was a very welcome piece of news. No
wonder he had been at such pains to assure her of
the inevitable failure of Grandmother's plans. But
he need not have been so obnoxious about it, she
thought scathingly.

'You're a nurse, aren't you?' Gran suddenly shot
out at her.

Sheena blinked. She could not see the connection,
and wondered if there was a little more to
Grandmother's request for her company. Was she

ill? 'Not quite,' she replied. 'I am in my last year. I was hoping to take my final exams in six months' time,' she added, seeing no harm in letting her newly-met relative know the facts of the matter.

'Who wants exams?' Grandmother said, off-handedly dismissing the subject, to Sheena's indignation. 'Wouldn't have got as far as you have if you weren't good at it,' she added sagely.

'That's not the point, Great-Grandmother,' Sheena said quickly. 'I must take my Finals, and I want to be a nurse.'

'Gran, if you please,' Gran Muldoon replied. 'Feel old enough as it is, without being reminded that I'm a great-grandmother. Look, you're young yet. Twenty-two, by my reckoning. Plenty of time to take those Finals if you still want to later, isn't there?'

Sheena drew in a deep breath. It was all so easy from Gran's point of view, but it would mean re-swotting and a lot of hard work before she sat for those finals. The longer she was away, the harder it would be for her. She had known all this before Matron at the teaching-hospital had pointed it out to her, but she had said that she would be quite willing to let Sheena come back to the hospital. They didn't like losing good nurses.

Seeing that the old lady was watching her, Sheena knew that it would be useless to argue this out with her. She had set her heart on keeping her with her, and even though Sheena knew that there was absolutely no hope of her cherished scheme being realised, she had to admit that she owed the old lady some consideration for the help she had given her family. She gave a small nod in answer to her Gran's query and left it at that.

'Then that's settled, then,' Gran Muldoon said with evident satisfaction, as if Sheena had made a wise choice. In reality she had had no choice at all, and Sheena was sure that the old lady was well aware of this. 'Now, I don't expect you to wait hand and foot on me,' she went on. 'I've got Milly to do that. She's been doing it for twenty years, and won't take kindly to being pushed into the background. You'll meet her later. I sent her out to do some shopping for me. You're not expected to do any skivvying either,' she assured the somewhat bemused Sheena. 'We've all the help we need in that line. All you have to do is to be nice to Brad, and things will turn out fine,' she added happily.

Sheena was by now even more incensed with Brad Muldoon. He had deliberately given her a false picture of what was expected of her, particularly the 'fetching and carrying' bit, knowing full well that this was done by this Milly person, whoever she was. She found this last ruling a bit much to take. 'In that case,' she said, with a glint in her green eyes, 'I might as well go back home!'

To her annoyance her Gran gave a deep-throated chuckle. 'That's just how it should be,' she said. 'Dislike him, do you?' There was a twinkle in her eyes.

Sheena's soft lips clamped together. 'I loathe him,' she declared flatly. 'I've never liked men who were too sure of themselves, and he's the worst example I've ever come across. I'm sorry, Gran, but if you're hoping for any romantic attachment between me and that man, you're backing a loser. He knows what you're up to, you know, and it's embarrassing for both of us. Well,' she conceded, 'me, anyway. I can't see him being embarrassed by anything.'

Far from disconcerting the old lady, these bold words seemed to produce an even brighter twinkle in her eyes. 'Course he's not embarrassed,' she said. 'He's a lawyer, isn't he? Take a lot to put him out of countenance, or make him show his feelings, come to that. I'm only taking a stab at how things are between him and Glenda Walling; he's tighter than a clam where his personal affairs are concerned.'

The name Glenda Walling produced a spark of interest from Sheena, as it would have done for most people. She was a well known socialite whose pictures appeared repeatedly in the high-society magazines, either attending charity balls or opening bazaars for good causes. Her father owned a chain of betting-shops and was reputed to be a multi-millionare.

This time the twinkle was in Sheena's eyes as she looked back at Gran. 'I'd say they were very well suited,' she commented, unable to keep a note of satisfaction out of her voice. She recalled a few spectacular divorce suits that Dean Walling had been cited in. What better prospects could Brad Muldoon have? He had probably received instructions from his prospective father-in-law. The way Dean Walling carried on, he would need a lawyer in the family!

As Sheena had regained her humour, Gran

Muldoon had definitely lost hers. 'Brad doesn't take divorce cases,' she said sternly. 'He's not Dean Walling's lawyer, and not likely to be either,' she added through stiff lips, 'so don't you go thinking on those lines, my girl. I've nothing against the daughter, it's the stock she comes from that I'm objecting to. Horse-traders, that's what they are, and always will be. That's how Dean Walling made his money, on the backs of punters from the betting-shops.'

At this point, a slight man with greying hair entered the room wheeling a trolley holding a tea-tray and plates of thinly cut sandwiches and cakes.

'Thank you, Stanley,' Gran said, as she cast an appreciative eye over the contents of the trolley. 'I like my tea,' she told Sheena, as she accepted the cup of tea that the man had poured out for her. 'Milly not back yet, I see,' she commented to the man now handing Sheena her tea. 'This is Sheena, Stanley. As I told you, she's come to live with us for a while.'

Stanley gave Sheena a slight bow, formal yet touching, and in a rather high voice said, 'Most suitable.'

Sheena, noticing that he had one blue eye and one brown one, found this phenomenon intriguing, as was the little man himself. His age was hard to determine, for he had round rather childish features, and could have been anywhere between thirty and fifty.

'More suitable than a Walling, eh, Stanley?' Gran asked drily, as she selected one of the tiny sandwiches from the plate held out to her.

'Most certainly,' replied the man, in a manner that startled Sheena in its intensity.

Her surprise was noted by her grandmother. 'Stanley's on our side, Sheena,' she confided. 'He's got personal reasons behind his dislike. All right, Stanley, we can manage now,' she said, and the little man, giving another of his quaint bows, left the room.

Sheena sat staring at the closed door after his departure. Did everyone in this house know why she was there? she wondered uncomfortably.

'Don't worry about Stanley,' Grandmother said airily. 'His family's been with the Muldoons so long that they consider themselves Muldoons, in fact, they are more proud of the name than we are.' She chuckled. 'Milly is Stanley's sister, and Mrs Cutter, our cook, is their aunt.' She reached out for another sandwich. 'For goodness' sake, girl, eat up! You make me feel greedy enjoying these sandwiches on my own,' she scolded.

Sheena obeyed the order. She was hungry, but events had somewhat taken the edge off her appetite. 'What personal reasons has Stanley got for disliking the Wallings?' she asked.

Her grandmother selected a cake, and indicated that Sheena should pour them out a second cup of tea. 'His father shot himself in one of their betting-shops. Couldn't pay his debts. Stanley felt they could have given him more time to pay. We would have seen him through, but his pride got in the way,' she added sadly.

There was a faint crash somewhere in the background just then, and Gran sighed. 'Milly's back' she said. 'I only hope that wasn't a piece of my best china.

If anyone was born with two left hands, Milly was.'

Sheena thought about this. She felt sorry for Stanley and his sister, but felt that it was unreasonable to hold the Wallings personally responsible for the tragedy. His father must have got himself pretty deep in debt to have reached that stage. But she held her own counsel.

Her thoughts turned eleswhere, something was niggling at the back of her mind, and then she knew what it was, something that Gran had said about Brad. She was afraid to put the next question for she felt that she knew the answer. 'Does Brad live here, or has he a flat near his work?' she asked.

Gran Muldoon gave her an odd sideways look. 'Here, of course!' she said, as if any other arrangement were unthinkable. 'So you'll be seeing a lot of him. Mind you, he's often late home, especially if he's a case on hand, and he's never back for lunch these days,' she added, with a trace of annoyance in her voice, 'and twice last week he was out to dinner somewhere, and that's what's worrying me. I suppose the next thing will be weekends spent at that fancy place over the hill where the Wallings have built that monstrosity of a building. More money than sense, if you ask me.'

Sheena's spirits lightened. From what little she had seen of Brad Muldoon, she felt confident that these absences of his would grow more frequent with her arrival in their midst, if only to prove to his grandmother that she was on a losing streak if she persisted with her scheme for Sheena's future. A future that he didn't want any part of. Neither, thank you, did Sheena herself, if it meant putting up with such an arrogant man!

CHAPTER TWO

TO SHEENA'S surprise, Brad Muldoon attended dinner that evening, and she did wonder whether it was his intention to discomfort her on her first evening at Grasslands. The house had taken the name of the old dairy farm that had brought the family so much prosperity in the past.

It was Milly who served them at table, and it was obvious that Brad was the apple of her eye. As she and her grandmother ate sparingly of each course, Sheena had ample opportunity to study points, and she unobtrusively watched the tall, gawky woman as she hovered around the table. Somewhere in her early forties, she could never, not even in her youth, have been attractive. Her large, bony features and dark brown eyes, too close together, gave her a clownish look. Nature, Sheena decided, had not been very kind to Milly, as far as physical attributes went.

Sheena wondered what Milly thought of her grandmother's grand scheme where she and Brad Muldoon were concerned, and suspected that his preference would come first with her, no matter what it was. Even a Walling, come to that!

The food was good, well cooked and presented, but Brad's presence made Sheena feel as if she was stealing every mouthful of the delicious veal blanquette, followed by a mouth-watering chocolate and rum charlotte sweet, as she met that icy blue stare of his across the table.

During the meal, conversation was sparse, which was just as well for Sheena, and she wondered if it was a rule not to indulge in chat while at the table. Although this was helpful, it was surprising how much could be conveyed by looks alone, she thought angrily, as she met that fixed blue stare with a glint of annoyance in her green eyes.

It was not until the meal was over, and coffee was served in the lounge, and Milly sent to clear the dinner dishes, that general conversation was indulged in, not by Sheena, but by Brad and his grandmother. It was Gran Muldoon who did most of the talking, with Sheena and Brad sizing each other up like a pair of prize fighters about to enter the ring.

'I shall be off to Lucy Wainwright's house Saturday afternoon,' Gran announced suddenly. 'She's one short for a hand of bridge. I dare say you can find time to take your cousin out for the afternoon, can't you?' she demanded.

Brad's scowl at this obvious play to throw them together was not lost on Sheena, who said hastily, 'Thank you, but I prefer to amuse myself; I——'

No one appeared to be listening to her, for Brad said angrily, 'You haven't been to a bridge party for months, why the sudden change? And I have plans for Saturday afternoon. It's Glenda's birthday, and they're having a barbecue in the grounds.'

This time it was Gran who put a spoke in before the end of Brad's sentence. 'Good, no reason why you shouldn't take Sheena with you, is there? If I know that sort of party, there'll be so many people

there one more won't make any difference, and it
will be a chance for Sheena to get to know a few
folk.'

In the midst of what looked like turning into a
heated argument, if Brad's scowl was anything to go
by, Sheena suddenly realised that tomorrow was
Saturday. 'Look, please, I'd rather not go out
tomorrow. I have to write to Mary, and I would like
some time to settle in, you know,' she pleaded.

'Nonsense!' Gran said firmly. 'You can write to
Mary this evening, can't you? In fact, you can do so
right now. You've everything you need in your
room, and I'm sure you could do with an early night
with all the travelling you've had to do.'

Sheena had no option but to obey her
grandmother's dictates in this matter, although she
would have preferred to argue the point. Feeling like
a teenager being sent to her room, she left them to
commence battle, for she was sure that Brad was in
no mood to comply with this latest whim of Gran
Muldoon's.

At least she was well out of that, she thought, as
she made her way to her room, but she was
determined to have her say in the matter when she
managed to get Gran on her own, for there were a
few points that her grandmother hadn't apparently
taken into account. For one thing, her one and only
summer suit, a cream linen, cut on severe lines,
might just be presentable at such an august
gathering, but it needed pressing, and on recalling
various society photographs, Sheena remembered
that hats were the in thing, she didn't feel that her
beret would fill the bill.

Sheena gave a sigh of exasperation. As if things weren't bad enough, now she had this to plague her. She did not want to go to that wretched barbecue any more than Brad wanted to take her, even had she had a wardrobe of dresses suitable for such an occasion. All this she would point out to her grandmother in no uncertain terms. Gran would have to learn that she was not a puppet on a string, that she had feelings, and there were limits to what could be expected of her.

The trouble was, these were not things to bring up in that wretched man's presence. If she had mentioned the question of suitable dress, he would have seen it as a blatant ploy to get her grandmother to fork out for a new wardrobe for her, and no way was Sheena going to allow him that satisfaction.

No, there were no two ways about it. She was not going to that barbecue, and even if Gran Muldoon managed to talk Brad into taking her, she would get him to drop her off somewhere in the city, and she could spend the afternoon shop-gazing and catch a taxi back around six. Gran wouldn't expect Brad to come back early, not just to give her a lift back; he would be spending the evening with his Glenda, wouldn't he?

Feeling that she had covered all points for any contingency, Sheena felt a little better, and sat down to write to Mary.

There was so much she could tell her, but in the end settled for a short missive to say that she had arrived, and gave her a description of the house, and Grandmother, of course, for, like Sheena, Mary had never met her great-grandmother. She omitted to mention Brad Muldoon. With any luck, Mary would never have cause to worry over his small-minded attitude towards the family. She had no idea how long her stay with the Muldoons would be, but she had a sneaking feeling that once Brad was safely married to his Glenda, she could expect to be on her way to complete her training. She did not, of course, say this to Mary; the less she knew of their grandmother's wild scheming on Sheena's behalf, the better. She just said that she didn't think it would be too long before she was home, and left it at that. Finally, she closed with a hope that Shaun was behaving himself, and not getting up to any pranks and upsetting Mary's husband Don. This however was hardly likely, as Don was a bit of a prankster himself, and if anything encouraged Shaun.

Once the letter was out of the way, Sheena lay down on her bed. She was tired, more tired than she had realised. She had been working nights lately at the hospital, and had only come off a night's duty to catch the coach to Canberra, so she prepared for bed, not wanting to be awakened in the morning lying on the bed still dressed.

As she crossed the passage to the bathroom opposite her bedroom, she thought how quiet the house was. No sounds came up from below, and she wondered how, or indeed whether, Gran had got her way in getting Brad to take her to the barbecue. She also wondered where Brad's room was, and devoutly hoped that it was in another section of the house. The place was large enough to hold another wing, separate from the main quarters. From what she had so far seen of Brad Muldoon, she was sure that privacy would be his first priority. She could no more see him share, or muck in for anyone's benefit, no matter what emergency arose, than she would imagine his being polite to her.

Sheena awoke to the tinkle of tea-cups, and sleepily acknowledged the tea-tray placed by her bedside by a solemn-looking Milly, who gave a slight nod of her head at Sheena's thanks, telling her that breakfast would be at eight-thirty.

Glancing at the clock by her bedside, Sheena saw that she had exactly half an hour's grace before presenting herself for breakfast, and settled back to enjoy her tea.

The tea was the only thing that she could enjoy when the events of the previous evening seeped back into her consciousness. The first thing she had to do was to have a talk with her grandmother, and somehow convince her that she had no wish to attend the barbecue. If the worst came to the worst, she could point out the salient fact that she had not come dressed for such an occasion. As it was the weekend, Sheena thought she could safely use this ploy without the risk of being embarrassed by any display of generosity on Gran's part. If that failed, then she would just have to fall back on her plan to get Brad to drop her off somewhere in the city, which no doubt he would be only too pleased to do.

To her relief, there was only her grandmother at the breakfast table, and no place laid for a third person. 'Brad's had his,' Gran Muldoon told Sheena as she saw her glance at his place opposite hers. 'He's had to go in to the office early, and no doubt pick up his gift for that Glenda' she added sourly. 'But what you get for a girl who's got everything, I can't imagine. Let's hope it's not an engagement ring.'

Sheena glanced down at the plate of eggs and bacon that Milly put before her, and waited until she was occupied at the sideboard with the coffee before saying mildly, 'Well, if it's what he wants, Gran, I don't see how you can change things. He's old enough to make up his own mind.'

'Maybe,' her grandmother said grudgingly, 'but it's all wrong. I feel it in my bones, and don't tell me I'm imagining things. I've had feelings like this before, and they're never wrong. You'll see.'

Sheena did not know whether she was imagining it, but it seemed to her that Milly's mouth had a grim look about it as she served them with coffee, and hovered about waiting to see if any more toast was needed, but she didn't really know Milly well enough to be sure about this.

'We can manage now, Milly. You'd be better be off on that errand I gave you. I said you'd be there before ten,' Gran Muldoon reminded her.

Now that Sheena had her grandmother on her own, she set about dissuading her from making Brad take her to the barbecue. 'I really do not want to go, Gran. I realise that you want me to meet people, but surely there's time enough for that? I shall be horribly miserable, you know, not knowing a soul there, and I'm certainly not tagging on to Brad. Not that he'd let me, you saw how keen he was to take me,' she added. 'I only hope he flatly refused. Did he?'

Gran Muldoon took a sip of her coffee, and fixed a faded blue eye on Sheena. 'Now, you're not going to let me down, are you?' she demanded. 'He's taking you, and you're going. I expect you'll enjoy it when you get there. A pretty girl like you will have no trouble in getting folk interested in you, particularly as you're related to Brad. That's as good as a dozen engraved calling cards. You'll see.'

Sheena felt very depressed. She couldn't see Brad exactly shouting the connection to all and sundry, quite apart from the fact that they couldn't stand each other. Added to that, her somewhat creased linen suit was hardly a recommendation for the proud Muldoons.

'If you're wondering what to wear, then don't. I've got a few things coming for you. That's where Milly's going, to pick them up. I ordered them last night from my dressmaker. Milly got your sizes from your coat and shoes in the wardrobe,' she added with a twinkle in her eyes. 'Any other objections?' she enquired mildly.

Sheena felt that she was up against a brick wall, and she couldn't even summon up a genuine thank-you for Gran's thoughtfulness, although she did try, but it came out very half-heartedly.

'I told you that I didn't expect you to spend your time keeping me company, didn't I?' Gran said drily. 'Look on it as a holiday. You're as good as those Wallings, better, in fact. You come from a long line of good blood, my girl. You show them.'

Sheena felt that this wasn't the time to remind her that she was a Fairburn, it wouldn't get her anywhere. She had tried that earlier, hadn't she? Well, she wasn't beaten yet. Her last plan could still work out, and she saw no difficulty in achieving Brad

Muldoon's co-operation in carrying it out.

She did not see Milly return, but shortly after breakfast her grandmother told her that her things had arrived, and no doubt she would like to try them on. Brad had said that he would be picking her up around eleven-thirty, and hoped that she would be ready. At least, that was the way her grandmother had put it, and Sheena could well imagine the manner in which the statement had actually been made. Be ready, or else!

With no great expectancy, Sheena took herself off to her room. If Gran had hoped that she would show more enthusiasm, then she was sorry to disappoint her, but though you could lead a horse to water, you couldn't make it drink, she told herself angrily, as she entered her room.

On the bed, wrapped in tissue paper was a peach-coloured dress, and, shaking it out of its wrappings, Sheena saw that it was full-skirted and had a scalloped neck, not too high nor too low, but just right. In fact, if Sheena would admit it, it was just the kind of dress she herself would have chosen, had she had the money to indulge herself in such an article of clothing. The sleeves she saw were long and buttoned at the wrist by six pearl buttons, and they reminded her of peaches and cream.

This, in fact, was certainly the colour scheme the dressmaker had in mind, for all the accessories were the same off-white colour as the buttons on the dress sleeves. Shoes, wide-brimmed hat with a slim peach ribbon to match the dress. White gloves and handbag completed the ensemble.

At any other time, Sheena would have been

delighted to wear the outfit, but her green eyes wore a cynical look as she stared at it, imagining Brad Muldoon's comments on first sight of her dressed to imitate high society.

Not that he would say anything in front of his grandmother. Oh, no! He would wait until they were alone, and then make some remark alluding no doubt to her hopes of getting herself accepted into society.

Sheena left it to the last possible moment before changing into her finery, feeling more like a shop dummy then Cinderella, and not even bothering to give herself a critical once-over in the mirror. She planted the hat on her head and grabbing the bag, made her way down to the hall where she found not only a scowling Brad waiting for her, but Gran as well, who exclaimed, 'You look a treat. I knew that colour would suit you. My word, and so it does!'

Brad's sneer and abrupt, 'Ready?' did not go unnoticed by a seething Sheena who nodded curtly and followed him out to the car in front of the house. It was not the Land Rover this time, but a Lancia, its bodywork gleaming in the sunshine.

Gran Muldoon's 'Enjoy yourselves' was lost in the roar of the car as it started up, but as neither of the occupants was in a mood to accept any such well meant advice, it was just as well.

'Feel good, do you?' Brad enquired in a sardonic tone, as the car swept out of the drive.

Sheena drew in a quick breath. Here it comes. He had hardly waited until they had cleared the grounds. 'Not really,' she replied. 'This wasn't my idea, if you remember. It was Gran's.'

'She's having a spate of these rotten ideas lately, isn't she?' he said caustically. 'Still, I don't suppose you're complaining. Got a nice outfit out of it, haven't you? Although clothes don't make the lady, you know.'

Sheena stared ahead of her. One more crack like that and she would hit him, driving or not! 'Look,' she said angrily, 'I don't want to go to this do any more than you want to take me. If you had had the guts to stand up to Grandmother in the first place I wouldn't be in this position, would I? So why don't we reach a compromise? Just drop me off in one of the shopping-areas of the city. I can browse around and go back this evening by taxi. Gran wouldn't expect you to bring me back, would she? And she wouldn't be any the wiser about it.'

'That's what you think!' Brad said sourly. 'Gran might have got a few bats in her belfry where you and I are concerned, but she's no fool. She'll ask questions that you'll get stuck to answer. No. You're going and I'm taking you, but don't hang around me, understand? That's as far as I'm going. Delivering you. The rest is up to you.'

'I could say that I kept well away from everybody, couldn't I?' Sheena persisted, not willing to lose her only chance of escape. 'Gran can ask what questions she likes, I'm sure I could think up some answers, and she couldn't be certain, could she?'

Brad gave her a sideways look that said more than words. 'And what do you think you'll look like parading the streets in that outfit?' he demanded. 'You look like a fashion-plate; folks will think you're a film star out for some publicity. No, you're coming with me, and that's an end to it!' he thundered.

Had Sheena's mind not been on other matters, she would have realised that Brad had unwittingly paid her a high compliment, but as it was, all she could see was that she would have to attend the barbecue, like it or not. As for his barbed comments on her not hanging around him, there was no fear of that. Once there, she intended to fade into the background, and stay long enough to prove her presence, then high-tail it back to Grasslands. There were sure to be plenty of taxis available with people coming and going, and she foresaw no difficulty there.

Eventually the car drew up in a large courtyard fronting a sprawling white mansion, and even though it was still early, there were plenty of cars already there. There was not a common make among them, Sheena noted with a sardonic twist of her soft lips.

After fumbling with the strange catch of the door to let herself out, with no assistance from the man at her side, who appeared to have his mind on other matters, Sheena scrambled out and waited for him to join her, feeling like a hitch-hiker who had just been picked up and helped a little along the journey.

'Straighten your hat!' Brad ordered, coming out of his reverie. 'It's supposed to be worn forwards, not on the back of your head like a sailor on leave.'

Sheena glared at him and tossed her head. 'I like it fine just how it is,' she spat out at him.

To her fury, Brad reached out a long arm and yanked the offending article forward, then nodding at the result, marched ahead of her towards a cool green awning that covered the whole front of the imposing residence.

Sheena was tempted to push the hat back to its original position, but thought better of it. It just wasn't worth it. He was obviously intent on preserving his dignity, in spite of having a poor relation in tow, although Sheena felt more like orphan Annie being led to meet her prospective relations, and put on her best behaviour.

The barbecue was being held at the back of the premises, and protected from the rays of the sun by the green canopy, Sheena followed Brad's tall back round the side of the house. The noise of clinking glasses and laughter grew louder as they approached the rear of the premises.

There were several shouted acknowledgements at Brad's arrival, and many curious glances at Sheena.

It was not hard to single out the birthday girl, who stood surrounded by a clutch of guests and dressed in what her brother Shaun would have described as her pyjamas. The sheer silk apricot two-piece with its wide ballooned sleeves that floated out as they caught the soft afternoon breeze presented a picture of serenity, emphasised by a white lace-brimmed hat perched demurely on golden hair, giving a suggestion of a halo.

Sheena was inclined to congratulate Brad on his choice of woman. Perfection in every line, she thought. As the lovely blonde now spotted their approach, the blue eyes lit up as if by a touch of a switch when they rested on Brad Muldoon, but took on a slightly darker hue when resting on Sheena.

'Happy birthday, darling,' Brad said in a soft

caressing tone, as he lightly touched the cherry-red lips lifted in expectation of the greeting.

Sheena felt like shaking her head. That couldn't be Brad Muldoon talking in that tone of voice, could it? She felt an insane urge to giggle, but hastily swallowed it back. He would kill her if she made him look a fool in front of this paragon.

'Glenda, this is Miss Fairburn,' he said, his tone almost back to normal as he recalled Sheena's presence, and all but thrust her forward to shake hands with Glenda, forgetting, Sheena noted with annoyance, to follow up the introduction for her benefit. But then, she didn't count, did she?

Glenda Walling's cool blue eyes did a quick survey of Miss Fairburn, as her hand barely touched Sheena's. 'How do you do,' she said in a smooth voice, and looked back at Brad. 'I don't remember seeing Miss Fairburn before, darling,' she said. 'Friend of yours?'

'Cousin,' Brad said abruptly. 'Distant connection,' he added for good measure. 'She's come to spend a week or two with us. You know how Gran is for family,' he tacked on meaningfully.

Sheena could have screamed. No doubt he would expand further on what he thought of his scrounging distant cousin, when they were alone. She wished that she could just walk away there and then. Just let Gran make any further plans for her to accompany this hateful specimen anywhere, she vowed silently, and she would be off home on the next train!

To make sure Sheena did not hang on to his coat-tails, Brad put himself out introducing her to all and sundry, in the hope, no doubt, that some good soul would monopolise her for the rest of the afternoon, and keep her out of his hair.

This was not difficult, for there were several bachelors on the look-out for any pretty girl, ideally on her own.

There were one or two, she noted, that he kept well clear of, obviously reasoning that Gran would not thank him for leading her to the local rakes.

A newcomer then loomed in sight, and it seemed to Sheena that Brad headed his way with almost undignifed haste. 'Leroy! I've been wondering where you'd got to,' he exclaimed, as they joined the man who was trying to catch the eye of the waiter with the drinks-tray.

'Hi, Brad. Got caught in one of those rotten traffic hold-ups. That's the worst of travelling midday Saturday. Well, who's this?' he asked, his eyes on Sheena who was trying to look invisible, and hovering behind Brad's broad back.

'Leroy, I want you to meet a distant cousin of mine. Miss Fairburn,' Brad replied, with no little relief in his voice. Sheena had no doubt at all that this was the person he intended to dump her on.

The said Leroy favoured Sheena with a knowing eye and held out his hand. 'Kept that pretty dark, didn't you, Brad?' he drawled suggestively as he held Sheena's hand in a grip that made her wince.

'I said distant cousin,' Brad answered with a trace of annoyance in his voice. 'Gran wanted to renew old ties, and you know what Gran is when she gets a bee in her bonnet. Look,' he said quickly. 'If you're a free agent, how about looking after Miss Fairburn for me? I'm a bit tied up right now.'

Sheena did not miss the gleam of surprised delight Leroy gave at this suggestion. 'Be happy to oblige,' he answered earnestly. 'You go off and placate your Glenda,' he added, with a wink at Brad which brought an annoyed frown to his features.

'Nothing like that about it,' he said abruptly, and made off in high dudgeon, heading in Glenda's direction.

'Well, now, let's get acquainted,' Leroy said happily as Brad disappeared from sight. 'I presume you have a Christian name,' he added with a grin.

Sheena did not much care for the way he was eyeing her with a proprietorial air, but had to reply. 'Sheena,' she said, in the tone of voice that warned him to watch his step.

'Ah, sounds Irish. Well, I'm just Leroy. Everybody calls me Leroy, even my mother, although I was christened Alphonso. Something to do with a book she was reading at the time, so I was given to understand. Would you like some refreshment? I see you haven't got a drink.' Before Sheena could reply he shouted at one of the waiters to bring some sustenance to two dehydrated souls, a request that sent up a shout of laughter from the other guests and made Sheena the object of curiosity from those she hadn't been introduced to.

By the time an hour had gone by, Sheena was at screaming-point. After eliciting what few facts she had wanted to give her enforced companion, he proceeded to give her a detailed account of his life history. This would have been fine had Sheena been at all interested, or indeed if there had been any interest in the tale, but as it was, Leroy appeared to have lived the very mundance existence of a socialite whose high spots of the year coincided with race meetings and outlandish parties given by associates. In a nutshell, Sheena had been landed with a crashing bore.

Without being too obvious, she had made several attempts at extricating herself from his company, but so far nothing had worked. She had paid one visit to the cloakroom, well signposted and in the large hall of the house, only to linger about there in hope that Leroy would find someone else to talk to, but he had stationed himself outside the house as if afraid Sheena would get lost on her way back to the barbecue. He was certainly taking his orders from Brad with a dedication that bordered on the ridiculous.

Sheena's chance came when he headed for the buffet after a shout of 'Tucker up!' ordering Sheena to stay right where she was.

There would never be another opportunity, Sheena was sure and she didn't intend to miss it. Brad Muldoon would have to give his apologies for her removal from the scene in whatever way he chose, she thought, as she slipped away from the milling crowd and made her way to what she hoped would be the gardens.

A dwelling of that size would have adequate grounds surrounding, it, she reasoned, and found that this was so, for soon she was wandering down trellis-covered walkways amid landscaped gardens. She had several hours to kill, so she was not worried about losing her way. Eventually she would reach the limits of the property, and then saunter back, taking her time and admiring the beauty of the flora around her.

It soon became apparant that she was in fact making a circle of the house, for after following several twisting paths that invariably branched off to the right, she found herself gazing out at a paddock sectioned off from the rest of the property by white railings.

Looking back, she saw that she had indeed done a circuit of the house, for a little further back from where she stood was a covered archway leading, she presumed, to the back quarters of the house, probably the stabling area.

At this point she heard the pounding of horses' hooves in the distance, and suddenly a rider came into sight, followed hotly by a second rider, in what must have been a race of some sort.

Sheena moved back towards the archway: she had no right to be there, barbecue or no barbecue, and had no wish to be accused of trespassing. With any luck, they would both depart as soon as they had appeared, she thought, and when all was clear she could go back the way she had come.

'Told you I could still do it, didn't I?' shouted the man who was the first in the paddock as he dismounted, and flung a careless pat at the sweating horse's flanks.

'All right, you've won your bet,' the second man said, as he dismounted. 'I'd have given you a better race if I hadn't eaten so much tucker,' he complained.

'I ate as much as you did,' the first man replied. 'No bones to pick there, old man, and you know it,' he added cheerfully.

Sheena moved a little further back into the recess of the archway then risked a quick glance out towards the paddock to where the men had been standing. She was dismayed to see that they were now heading her way and would soon reach the archway. Now she had no choice but to remain hidden from view, and blessed the shadows cast by the sun that gave her some cover.

They had almost reached the archway when one of the men suddenly exclaimed, 'Blast! I've left my jacket by the fence. You go on, Dave, I'll catch you up. Line up a large scotch for me.'

Sheena moved closer to the wall of the archway as the man called Dave strode past her, hardly giving a glance in her direction, his heavy breathing showing that he was still recovering from the gallop, and Sheena gave him a second's start before she glanced back at the paddock fence.

'Oh, my word, my word!' the hoarse cry reached Sheena as she moved out of her cover and looked towards the paddock, then back again at the man who had just passed her and was well in front of her and about to disappear round the bend leading to the back premises. The fact that he kept on going made it obvious that he had not heard his companion's cry.

Sheena had no choice but to go to the man's assistance, and found him half sitting, half lying on the grass by the fence.

'Get Dave,' the man said breathlessly,' and find Glenda, she'll know what to do.'

Sheena's fingers went to the man's pulse. It was a

natural action on her part, and her training as a nurse now took over.

When she was satisfied that the patient had not suffered a heart attack, she competently loosened the man's tie, and helped him into a more comfortable position. 'Just sit quietly,' she said 'You'll be right in a moment.'

The man gave her a hard look. 'You a doctor?' he asked, his breath coming more normally now.

Sheena shook her head. 'No, a nurse,' she replied, then added, 'Well, almost. I've got to take my Finals first. If you still want a doctor to see you, I'll go and find Glenda for you.'

With a shake of his leonine head, the man took a deep breath and stood up, towering over Sheena who thought that he must be at least six feet two. 'You'll do for me,' he said in a dry voice. 'Guess I panicked back there. Sure thought I'd had it that time. Serve me damn well right. I had no business galloping at that speed at any time, let alone after a heavy meal.' He stared at Sheena. 'I don't recall seeing you around before.'

By now, Sheena had realised that the man was Dean Walling, Glenda's father, and explained her presence. 'I'm from Victoria,' she said. 'A friend brought me,' and left it at that, not wanting to identify the 'friend'. He wasn't a friend at all, she thought sourly, quite the reverse, in fact, as she recalled the way he had dumped her on the town bore.

'Well, welcome to Canberra, Miss Victoria,' he said, obviously quite recovered, judging by the glint in his dark eyes.

'It's Fairburn, actually,' she said.

'I prefer Victoria,' he replied. 'You look like a Victoria to me, and I'm mighty grateful to you. That fool of a doctor would have had me under wraps by now and out of circulation for the rest of the season, if I know him. 'You'll dine with me tonight,' he said. It was not an invitation, but an order.

Sheena blinked in amazement. 'I'm afraid that's out of the question,' she said haughtily, resenting the way that Dean Walling had anticipated no refusal to his summons. 'I dine with my grandmother,' she said, seeing with some amusement his astonishment at her flat refusal. 'I always dine with my grandmother,' she added for good measure.

Dean stared at her. He was not too sure that she wasn't having him on. This was not an excuse that he had anticipated; indeed it was the only time he had ever met it. A refusal in itself was unusual enough. Whatever problems he might have had with the opposite sex, this was not one of them. The problems usually came when he had lost interest in his current fancy, and this was where the cheque book came in handy. 'Supposing I had a word with your grandmother?' he asked, with a challenging light in his eyes. 'I could explain that I only wished to repay the charming young lady who had saved my life.'

Sheena's eyebrows rose. 'What nonsense!' she exclaimed. 'Saved your life, indeed! You had simply overeaten, and then taken a gallop on a full stomach. No doubt your doctor would have told you that anyway,' she added drily.

'Oh, no, he wouldn't,' Dean replied loftily. 'You

know my doctor. You saved me a packet just by using those lily-white hands of yours.' At this he caught Sheena's hand and placed it to his lips.

The action embarrassed Sheena, who turned a bright pink, much to the amusement of Dean Walling.

'I'm going to see more of you,' he said, 'grandmother or no grandmother. Where did you say you were staying?'

Sheena hadn't said, and she had no intention of saying either. She could just imagine Gran's annoyance should Dean Walling turn up on the doorstep requesting her company! It would start a full-blooded feud! Not only was Dean's daughter threatening to snatch Brad away from the family, but Dean's chasing Sheena, who was supposed to save him from such a fate, would be too much for Gran to stomach!

'I don't think I'll tell you that,' she said with a trace of waspishness in her voice.

'And why not, may I ask?' Dean demanded in an arrogant voice, but the twinkle in his eye belied the severity of his tone.

'Because she's getting on, and too much excitement is bad for her,' Sheena replied exasperatedly.

Dean burst out into delighted laughter. 'So you know who I am,' he said,' and no doubt your Gran does, too,' he added in high amusement.

Sheena acknowledged this with a small, curt nod.

'All right. I promise not to disclose our association if you'll promise to dine with me on Monday, otherwise I shall be forced to march up to your door and demand your attendance.

Sheena stared at him. 'That's blackmail!' she said

indignantly.

'Yes, I know, but how else am I going to see you again?' he said slyly. 'I can always find out where you are staying, you know. I do have your name. Come on, just one dinner-date, that's all I'm asking for, and I promise to behave myself.'

Sheena drew a deep breath. It wasn't going to be easy, and it would mean telling a fib and making up some story to tell Gran. On the other hand, if he carried out his threat of turning up on the doorstep, and she was in no doubt that he would do just that; he was the type of man who intended getting his own way by fair means or foul. It was true that he had her name and a few enquiries would soon produce the necessary information for him to act on. Sheena had no choice in the matter.

'Well?' Dean demanded aggressively.

'Very well,' Sheena said, 'Monday evening,' and at the sudden grin this capitulation produced, added swiftly, 'Not at your home. Somewhere quiet,' she stipulated, not wanting to run into Brad who just might be dining there too.

'You mean somewhere where no one knows me?' he said with an even wider grin. 'I'm not sure that's going to be easy, but I can always hire a room where we can dine in peace.' He then gave her a mock salute. 'Till Monday, Victoria. I shall pick you up outside Parliamant House at seven-thirty. They run half-hourly tours so you have a good excuse for going there, in case of difficulty. Now I must make myself presentable for the party.' Giving her another mock salute, he left her.

CHAPTER THREE

SHEENA was half-way back to the barbecue when Leroy pounced on her. 'I've been looking for you everywhere!' he exclaimed. 'There was I was with two great whacking helpings of roast lamb and no sign of you!'

'Sorry,' Sheena said 'but I'm not used to crowds and suddenly wanted to get away, so I explored the gardens.'

She most certainly had wanted to get away, but mostly from the man who was now deciding whether to accept her apology. He evidently did, for he caught hold of her arm in an annoying proprietorial fashion, and escorted her back to the party.

'I know how you feel,' he confided. 'Can't stand crowds myself. What say we go off somewhere on our own? We can have dinner later at a little restaurant I know quite near the city parks.

Sheena had not been exactly thrilled at the idea of having dinner with Dean Walling, and she was even less thrilled at the thought of having dinner with Leroy. She was about to give the same excuse that she had given Dean about always taking dinner with her grandmother, when a thought struck her. Her association with Leroy could be useful. Brad knew Leroy, and would no doubt welcome him, or anyone, come to that, who proved a diversion from Gran's schemes. All she need say on Monday was that she was

47

dining out, and both Gran and Brad would presume she was with Leroy. She absently nodded at this perfect solution to her problem, then replied, 'I think I should like that. I haven't had much time to see the city.'

A delighted Leroy guided her to his car, and, telling Sheena that really no one would miss them, and that he didn't fancy charging through the crowd to bid their hostess farewell, he settled her in his two-seater sports coupé. With a roar of the powerful engine he swept her away from the party.

All the rest of that afternoon, and the dinner that evening, Sheena had to keep reminding herself that however much of Leroy's constant verbosity on the importance of Leroy she had had to put up with, it was all in a good cause. She did give a sigh of thankfulness when at last he dropped her at Grasslands later that evening, and managed not to commit herself to another evening of purgatory by vaguely murmuring, 'See you.' Before he could make any attempt at a more affectionate farewell she held out her hand for him to take, and drew it smartly away before he got any other ideas.

As she went through to the lounge, Sheena half expected to find Gran waiting up for her, though it was long past her bedtime. She was relieved when she found an empty lounge. She met Milly on her way out, who enquired politely if she had enjoyed herself, to which she replied untruthfully, 'Very much, thank you.' Turning down a nightcap, she went straight to bed.

The bright sunlight awakened Sheena the following morning, and she lay for a few moments collecting her senses as she recalled that it was Sunday and breakfast would be taken at nine, giving her an extra half-hour in bed.

She did not feel particularly bright, in fact her head felt heavy and she suspected she would be starting the day with a headache. Little wonder, she thought, remembering Leroy's endless diatribe on the subject of Leroy. She silently vowed never to let herself in for another evening like that.

Her thoughts went from Leroy to Brad Muldoon. He must have known full well what a crashing bore Leroy was, and had Sheena needed any confirmation on this point, she had received plenty of evidence to support this theory during the afternoon and evening in his company. Not once had they been approached by any of the other guests at the barbecue. In fact, looking back, Sheena could now see that a purposeful distance was kept by the rest of the assembly. For good reason, as Sheena had learnt to her cost.

That was one more black mark to be added to Brad Muldoon's account, she thought darkly. She hoped that some day, somehow, she would be able to even up the score, which was all a little one-sided if not definitely overweighted on his side of the scales.

At breakfast, as Brad had predicted, Gran was full of questions. How had she enjoyed herself? Who had she met?

Sheena had not missed the smug expression on Brad's face as these questions were put to her, and recalling the dinner-date she had to keep on Monday, she decided to play her part and give an convincing display for both their benefits. 'I quite enjoyed it, Gran,' she said, hoping she sounded brighter than she felt. 'I can't remember who I met, there were so many, and Brad introduced me to Leroy, who very kindly kept me company, and took me out to dinner after a stroll round the city park.'

Gran gave Brad a long hard look, which told Sheena that Gran had heard of Leroy.

'She was safe enough with Leroy,' said Brad defensively, in answer to the look he had received from Gran. 'There were the usual hangers-on there, waiting to pounce on any unescorted female,' he added for good measure.

'Hmph!' growled Gran, not at all placated.

'He's a good enough chap, really. Apt to talk a bit too much, but otherwise harmless,' Brad pointed out.

'Oh, yes,' Sheena agreed quickly, too quickly, for she got a suspicious look from Brad at her enthusiasm. Don't overdo it, she reminded herself, or he'll spot you're up to something. 'Well,' she conceded, 'I hate crowds, you know, and social gatherings aren't my scene, so I was really grateful when he suggeested that we left the party and had a look round the parks.'

Brad's look of suspicion was now replaced by his usual sneering one. 'He's quite well off, too,' he said to no one in particular. His point was well taken by both his listeners.

'Sheena's not looking for a millionaire,' Gran said sharply. 'She's more sense than that, I know. Money's all right in proportion, but it won't buy happiness. Look at the Wallings. That Dean Walling in particular. He's always in some scrape or other, mostly through women. If he wasn't as rich as he is, he wouldn't be able to carry on the way he does.'

Brad threw down his napkin in a gesture that said more than words. 'Glenda can't be blamed for her father's shortcomings,' he said curtly. 'She's as worried about his way of life as any good daughter would be, and goes on hoping he'll eventually settle down.'

Sheena kept her eyes on the breakfast table, feeling distinctly uncomfortable, and hoping that no one would notice. She wondered what both of them would have said had they known that she was due to take dinner with the person now under discussion. As for Gran's certainty that she wasn't looking for a millionaire, Dean Walling was reputed to have several millions.

After Brad had stalked off in a huff, Gran and Sheena settled themselves in the lounge, Gran picking up her crochet, and Sheena idly glancing through the papers.

'You can't really like that Leroy,' Gran said suddenly. 'He's only put up with because of his family's city connections. The man's an ass, and a bore into the bargain. Were you trying to rile Brad by pretending to like him?' she asked.

Sheena glanced up from the article she was reading. Gran was no fool, she thought. 'Not really,' Sheena replied, hoping to be forgiven for the lie. 'Let's put it this way, Gran. I was grateful to him. I didn't want to go, you know, and I haven't a lot in common with the type of guest that goes to those functions. If it hadn't been for Leroy, I would really have felt out of my depth.'

Gran sighed. 'You've a lot more sense than Brad, that's for sure,' she said. 'What does he want with that crowd? Not a worth-while life between them. Always attending some party or other. Say it's for a good cause, well, I suppose some of the charities do well out of them, but as far as they're concerned it's just an excuse for having a good time. You wouldn't get any of them knuckling down to do any real work.'

Sheena went back to her paper. The thought of her coming date with Dean Walling now filled her mind, and made her feel wretched at the deception. She hoped Dean would find somewhere where he would not be recognised, but the chances of this happening were remote. All she could do was to trust to luck.

Once that obligation was fulfilled, she would have no further worries on that score. She was too fond of Gran to go on deceiving her.

'One good thing,' Gran said, sorting out her pattern for reference, 'he's not asked her to marry him yet. I was afraid that it was an engagement ring that he had in mind for her birthday present.'

Sheena sighed inwardly. Much as she disliked Brad Muldoon, she could feel sorry for him as far as his choice of woman went. She knew that he was very fond of his grandmother, and suspected that this was the sole reason for his tardiness in proposing to the woman he had set his heart on. If only Gran could be made to understand that dreams were one thing and reality another. There was also the fact that she didn't, and never would, like the man Gran had chosen for her to marry.

'It must be very hard for Brad,' she began hesitantly, and at Gran's surprised look at this statement, went on, 'He's very fond of you, you know, and I don't think he would do anything to cause you any unhappiness. But don't you see, he really does care for Glenda, and from what I saw of her, I believe she feels the same way about him. Why not give them your blessing?' she urged earnestly.

Gran stared at her as if she had taken leave of her senses. 'Because it will be harder for Brad in the long run if I don't bring him to his senses,' she stated firmly. 'Of course the girl's in love with him. I can give you any number of girls, daughters of my acquaintances, who have gone overboard for him. Guess I wouldn't have been exactly pleased if he had settled for any of them, but he won't get mixed up with that Walling ménage if I've anything to do with it.'

Sheena knew that she had come up against a stone wall, a solid stone wall of prejudice. No matter what, Gran was not about to abandon her pipe-dreams. She drew in a deep breath. If she were Brad, she would skip off to the nearest registrar's office and complete the deed, then confront Gran with the fact. Only then would she have to give way. Someone had to eventually, and she couldn't see Brad Muldoon giving in to what he considered a spate of crazy ideas on Gran's part. They were crazy, too, Sheena acknowledged. Whatever else she felt about him, they were as one on this particular issue!

Brad did not put in another appearance that day. 'Out at that Glenda's, no doubt,' Gran said, frowning at his empty place at lunch.

For her part, Sheena welcomed his absence, and spent the early evening with Gran reminiscing about old times, and feeling more of a traitor as the hours crept nearer the following day when she had to keep her dinner appointment.

Leroy rang just before six-thirty, inviting her out to dinner, but Sheena, taking the call in the hall, put him off with a suggestion for perhaps an evening next week, and left it at that.

'Who was that?' Gran asked, when she rejoined her in the lounge.

'Leroy,' Sheena answered. 'Wants to take me out to dinner tonight, but I put him off till tomorrow.'

Gran's lips puckered in disapproval at this news, but she said nothing, and Sheena was relieved that it had been so easy to solve her problem of dining out on Monday. There was another little problem however, to be surmounted. If Leroy was to take her out to dinner, he would be expected to pick her up at Grasslands, and somehow she had to get to Parliament House under her own steam.

This little problem nagged at her during dinner, until she suddenly recalled Dean saying that tours were arranged for Parliament House. Why shouldn't she say that she would like to take one of those tours? She could leave early in the afternoon, couldn't she? And say that she would arrange to meet Leroy in the city.

In the event, she found that she had been worrying unnecessarily over Gran's reaction to her proposal. Gran might suggest that there was plenty of time to take in such tours, but she was surprisingly enthusiastic over the idea, and welcomed the fact that Sheena showed an interest in the running of the country. She was sorry that she couldn't accompany her, but she would get Stanley to take her there, giving Sheena a few uncomfortable moments until Gran added that he would have to come straight back as he had the lawns to do that afternoon.

So far, things were working out nicely for Sheena. She hoped that they continued to do so. This was the first time, and most certainly the last, that she would indulge in subterfuge; it simply wasn't worth it.

The only good thing about the afternoon was that she would actually take one of the tours, and could truthfully tell Gran about it afterwards. This cleared her conscience a little on the way to the city, with Stanley pointing out places of interest as they swept along Commonwealth Avenue.

Sheena spent an interesting afternoon, not only at Parliament House, but taking in the Royal Australian Mint, where she watched money being made, then she had tea in one of the numerous cafés bordering the park. Had she not been full of apprehension about her coming meeting with Dean Walling, she would have thoroughly enjoyed the outing.

The trouble was, things had gone too smoothly, and going by the old adage that crime didn't pay, she felt certain that somewhere there would be a fly in the ointment. She was convinced that it would appear some time during the evening with Dean.

As things turned out, the fly, or hitch, appeared a little earlier than she had bargained for. She had got back to Parliament House just after seven, and joined the rest of the sightseers still milling around the lobby, so she did not feel conspicuous. She would stroll outside around seven thirty, hoping, it must be said, that Dean Walling had forgotten the appointment.

Her attention was on a notice board when a voice behind her made her nearly jump out of her skin. 'Getting some culture, are you?'

Sheena turned to face Brad. The thought raced through her mind, how long was he going to be there? Please goodness he would be gone before Dean Walling arrived to pick her up!

She was still gathering her wits when he added silkily, 'Gran's idea, was it? Hoping to get you familiar with my line of country?'

Sheena's lovely eyes opened wide as the possibility occurred to her, but it hadn't before. No wonder Gran was so amenable about her taking the tour! She had been too relieved at reaching her goal even to wonder at her co-operation!

'Actually, no,' Sheena said angrily. 'It was my idea, not Gran's. I hadn't connected your work with it, believe it or not,' she added.

'Of course not,' he replied sarcastically. 'By the way, I hope you're not relying on my giving you a lift home. I'm picking Glenda up in half an hour.'

Sheena's hands curled into small fists by her side. So that was what he thought, was it? She had been hanging around in the hope of running into him. No doubt he thought that Gran had told her the time he usually left his office. 'I had no such thought in mind,' she replied angrily. 'I'd rather rely on the taxi service. In any case, I'm dining with Leroy this evening, and won't be going back until later.' She was unable to suppress a note of satifaction in her voice. It wasn't often that she could slap him down, and she couldn't resist making the most of it. Put that in your pipe and smoke it, she almost added.

'You've not met Leroy's mother, have you?' Brad said with an air of smugness. 'She's a great stickler for family connections. I'm afraid yours wouldn't measure up to her standards of what she's in mind for Leroy. So don't say I didn't warn you.' He strode off through the exit.

Sheena found herself actually trembling with rage. Of all the rotten, low-down, hateful characters, he took the cake! Oh, she'd get even with him one day, just see if she didn't!

By the time Dean collected her, Sheena had reached the stage of not caring who saw her in his company. She was sorry about disappointing Gran, but there was a limit to what she was prepared to put up with out of gratitude.

In fact, she decided, it would be better for all concerned if she *was* found out. At least, she would be able to enjoy herself without this sneaking feeling of treachery hovering over her. She was almost sorry when Dean remarked airily that he had managed to find somewhere where they would not be disturbed, so she need have no worries on that score.

'Not that I approve of going about things this way,' he said, glancing at her swiftly. 'I like to show off my women,' he added.

This brought Sheena back to reason faster than anything else could have done. 'I'm not one of your women!' she snapped back at him.

Dean gave her another swift glance. 'Not yet,' he

said meaningfuly, 'but you'd be surprised to know how much I've been thinking about you all the weekend.'

Sheena stared out at the passing landscape, which seemed vaguely familiar, and thought of the type of woman he usually associated with. Socialites with money to burn, and here she was, in her cream linen suit that could be picked up in any leading store for a modest amount. She glanced down at it. She had Milly to thank for pressing it, she thought, although she hadn't asked her to. As for Dean thinking about her all the weekend, she wasn't going to fall for that one. He was just trying to flatter her, she thought grimly.

As the large cream Rolls swept into a drive, Sheena knew why the scenery had seemed familiar to her. He had brought her to his home! 'I thought——' she began angrily.

'Hold it,' Dean said, in some amusement. 'We're not there yet. Wait and see.'

The car swept majestically past the large white structure of the house, and continued on its way, taking a circular tour of the grounds, eventually drawing up beside a long low cabin affair, set in woods, some distance from the house, and completely isolated from the outside world.

'This,' he said to Sheena, 'is my domain. Nobody, but nobody, is allowed to set foot in this place without my permission. There are times when I need privacy, and this is the only way I can guarantee it.' He produced a key from his pocket and unlocked the heavy-looking oak door, and ushered Sheena in.

She found herself in a long room that looked as if it might run the length of the building. It was furnished with white leather furniture, with a bar at the end of the room. It occurred to Sheena that even in seclusion, Dean intended to live in comfort.

A large stone fireplace with a log-filled grate waiting the touch of a match was the finishing touch. Either Dean or one of his servants had prepared it for the evening.

'Come into the kitchen,' Dean said, leading the way through the door on the right of the lounge into a passage.

Sheena had another surprise when she saw the kitchen. It was large and contained every conceivable device a modern housewife needed to make her life easier.

Dean walked over to a large white cabinet and raised the lid to reveal a deep-chested refrigerator. 'We'll select our dinner from here,' he said. 'There's a list of contents at the side. All we have to do is pop them into the microwave and lay the table.'

A bemused Sheena chose an egg mayonaise for her starter, and lamb cutlets with all the trimmings as her main course. Dean selected steak, preferring a slice of melon for his starter.

With practised ease, Dean got the meal under way, then taking a lovely refectory table from its position along the wall at one side of the lounge, and placing it opposite the fireplace, he set the places for the meal, using beautiful hand-carved table-mats to protect the gleaming surface of the table.

Just before the meal was ready, he set the fire

alight and soon the logs were blazing in the hearth.

Sheena, watching all this, had a suspicion that this
was not the first time Dean had entertained someone
to dinner. It was all too pat, the actions had
obviously been well rehearsed. But that was nothing
to do with her, she reminded herself sharply, and it
never occurred to her that, considering all that she
had heard and read about the legendary Dean
Walling, she should have been a trifle wary at
finding herself alone with him. Strangely, no such
worry was in her mind; she felt as safe as she would
have done dining with an old friend.

As neither wished to sample the exotic cream
pastries provided for the sweet, they settled for fresh
fruit. After the meal, during which Dean made small
talk on general subjects of no significance, Sheena's
offer to tackle the washing-up as her contribution
was waved away by his casual remark that he
possessed a dish-washing machine. In any case, his
man would see to all that. This saved any further
argument on this score, and they took their coffee
comfortably seated in front of the blazing fire.

Sheena, sipping the excellent coffee, and feeling
very relaxed, was quite unprepared for Dean's
sudden turn to more personal matters.

'I suppose your grandmother doesn't approve of
Glenda, either, does she?' he asked casually.

Sheena blinked in astonishment at the question,
then when she had recovered she replied, 'So you
know who I am?'

Dean nodded, his brown eyes alight in
amusement.

'Does Glenda know that I'm dining with you

tonight?' Sheena asked, dreading the reply, for what Brad Muldoon would have to say about that she hated to think. She could not see Glenda keeping such news to herself.

'Certainly not!' Dean said firmly. 'When I knew who you were, I was able to appreciate your wish for anonymity. She will not know until I decide otherwise,' he added meaningly.

Sheena was grateful for this at least, but she hadn't liked the bit added on the end. 'Thank you,' she said, deciding not to probe further.

'So I was right,' he said, 'about your grandmother not caring for Brad Muldoon's interest in my daughter.'

Sheena saw no reason why she should evade the question. Dean was an intelligent man, and would not appreciate being side-tracked. 'I suppose you could put it that way,' she said, adding quickly, 'I'm sure she'll eventually come round to accepting the fact that they care for one another.'

Dean took Sheena's empty cup from her, and poured them both a refill. 'Do they?' he asked with lifted brows.

Accepting the cup from him, Sheena frowned. That was an odd thing to say, surely? 'Well, I thought they did,' she said, 'and by the way Gran worries over the association, I'd say they do.'

'Ah, but you don't know Glenda, do you?' he commented musingly. 'Don't really know Brad Muldoon either, do you?' he added.

Sheena's green eyes glinted. She knew as much about that man as she wanted to know, and that was quite enough for her! Before she got into deep waters, she felt she ought to clarify a few things. 'What did Glenda say about me?' she asked.

Dean grinned. 'Wasn't much she could say, was there?' he replied. 'All she knew was that Brad turned up with a lovely woman in tow and said that you were a distant cousin of his. I'm not too sure if Glenda swallowed it, but she seemed to take comfort from the fact that you spent the afternoon with Leroy. How on earth did you get lumbered with him?'

'Brad introduced me to him,' Sheena replied.

'How very unkind of him,' Dean commented with a wicked grin, 'and Glenda would take the view that if you were an old flame of Brad's he was doing his best to ditch you.'

Sheena, catching the amusement in his voice, had to smile. It all made sense, but she was surprised that Brad had not confided in Glenda and told her what he thought of his scrounging cousin.

'I don't think your grandmother has much to worry about,' Dean said, breaking into Sheena's thoughts. 'Glenda might want Brad, but he's no fool. He's attracted to her, of course, what male wouldn't be? She's a beauty, takes after her mother, but I only wish she had her mother's temperament to go with the looks.'

There was silence for a second or so, then he said, 'I suppose it's my fault really. I spoilt her. She was all I had, you see. She's never been denied anything. Whatever she wanted she got.' He leaned forward, and pushed a log that was threatening to fall into the hearth back into position. 'But Brad Muldoon's his own man. As Glenda knows what she wants, so does he, and that doesn't make for happiness in the long run.'

He glanced at Sheena whose eyes were on the leaping flames of the fire. 'She was disappointed not to get an engagement ring for her birthday, you know, but it confirmed my thoughts on the matter. Brad Muldoon's just playing with her.' He gave a wry grimace. 'I've no right to criticise anyone on those grounds,' he stole another quick glance at Sheena, 'but I recognise the tactics well enough. You don't know Brad, as I said, but I can assure you that once a man of his calibre makes up his mind wild horses wouldn't drag him from his goal.'

Sheena looked at him. What he had said seemed hard to believe, but, as little as she knew Brad Muldoon, she had a feeling that Dean was right about him. She had thought it was her grandmother who was holding up the affair, but now, when she came to think about it, it couldn't have been. As Dean had said, Brad wasn't the type to bow to anyone's dictates, not even his grandmother's, fond as he was of her.

She sighed. 'Oh, dear,' she said. 'Poor Glenda.'

Dean studied her for a moment. 'Poor Glenda, as you put it, has had it coming for quite a while,' he said drily. 'She's been breaking hearts since she was sixteen. Off with the old, on with the new, has been her life-style, I'm afraid. Don't you see,' he said, 'that's why she's really keen on Brad? She senses the truth but refuses to believe it. He's a challenge to the feminine wiles that have never failed her before, and she doesn't intend them to fail now.'

After coffee, Dean offered Sheena a liquer, but she turned it down, mainly because she wanted to keep a clear head.

She found that she was liking Dean Walling very much, and an old saying went through her mind, 'Not as black as he's painted'. She was also curious about him; he didn't seem at all the type of playboy the papers had dubbed him. 'What happened to your wife?' she asked quietly.

Dean helped himself to a whisky and soda, offering Sheena anything she fancied, and she settled for dry sherry. 'Well, it was a long time ago,' he replied, handing her a sherry and returning to his seat opposite her. 'She was a racing enthusiast, cars, not horses,' he explained. 'Went on one of those crazy overland races where anything goes, there's no rules, and glory the other end if you pull it off.' He took a sip of his drink. 'Tried to avoid running into a pack of dingos on a fast straight run. She didn't make it.'

Sheena glanced down at her sherry. 'I'm sorry,' she said in a low voice, there wasn't much else she could say.

'It was a long time ago,' he said. 'Sure, it set me back in my tracks for a while, but one day you wake up and decide that life's worth living.' He grinned at Sheena. 'Very much worth living,' he added meaningfully. 'Now it's your turn. I know you're a nurse. Well, almost,' he added, as Sheena started to correct him, 'and that you're on a visit to Canberra, that's all.'

Sheena found herself telling Dean all about her family and how she came to be in Canberra, only

leaving out the reason for Gran's sudden wish for
company. 'She's getting old,' she said, 'and wanted
to see me. She's trying to bring the family together,
but I think it's a little too late for that. We've led an
entirely different life, and I feel awkward with so
much wealth around me.' She wondered why she
had said that; it was the truth, but not the sort of
thing you told a comparative stranger. 'Anyway,'
she added quickly, 'I shall be off home again as soon
as I get the opportunity. I hope it won't be too long,
as I've some studying to get through before I take
my Finals.'

Dean looked at her, his eyes travelling slowly over
her oval face, and lingering on her eyes. 'Is that
what you really want?' he said. 'Spending the rest of
your life marching up and down hospital wards? Oh,
I know it's a worthy cause, and someone has to do it,
but I don't think it's for you, Victoria. You ought to
have a husband and children to look out for. I gather
there's no one in the background?' he asked
suddenly.

A startled Sheena blinked in astonishment. What
an extraordinary thing to say! 'No, there isn't,' she
said indignantly, 'and I'm not too sure that there
ever will be.'

'Taken a toss, have you?' Dean asked in amusement. 'Then he's a fool,' he said, 'but I'm grateful
to him.'

Sheena decided to ignore this last remark. 'Not a
fool,' she replied, 'just ambitious.'

'Even more of a fool, then,' Dean growled. 'It's
the worst reason of all, and one soon regretted.'

Her thoughts went back in time, and with a spurt

of surprise she found that the man whom she had
thought she was in love with now appeared as a
shadowy figure in the background, of no con-
sequence, merely a youth of her acquaintance. Her
eyes traced the features of the man now watching
her, seeing the touches of grey appearing at the
temples. Around forty-two, she surmised, but his
own man, and one not likely to be swayed by the
opinions of others.

'And now you're stuck with Leroy,' he said,
breaking into her thoughts.

Sheena was about to deny this when he added,
'You are stuck, you know. I can't see Leroy letting
go once he's got you in his sights. He's not exactly
overloaded with personal friends.'

As things stood, Sheena was well aware of this. 'I
could always get an urgent call home,' she said
drily, although this was hardly likely. It had
occurred to her that if things got too impossible she
could always send Mary an SOS to invent some
reason for her to return home.

Dean looked at her. 'Now if it were only Leroy
you were stuck with, I would say that was a wise
move, but now there's me. I've got to arrange for us
to meet in public and just go on from there. Leroy
won't get a look in, I can assure you, and I've no
intention of letting you go out of my life now that
I've found you. Besides, I've too much on at the
moment to go haring off after you, but I will do so if
necessary.'

Sheena was still thinking about his remarks on
arranging for them to meet in public. He really
didn't expect her to agree to that, surely? Not after

all the trouble she had taken to avoid it. She shook her head vehemently. 'I thought you understood why I wanted to keep this meeting from Gran,' she said crossly.

Dean grinned at her. 'You know, I don't think you know your grandmother, either. From all I've heard she's a lady who will take everything in her stride. She might be old, but she's a battler through and through. She won't thank you for mollycoddling her.'

Sheena looked away from his searching gaze. There was no doubt that he was right. Gran was a battler, but there was more to it than that. She could hardly tell him exactly what Gran was battling for! She sighed inwardly. Things were getting more and more complicated, and she didn't see how they could be resolved. All she could do was stick to her original thoughts on the matter, and keep away from Dean, even though she liked him a lot. 'You're forgetting your reputation,' she said, hating what she had to do, but somehow she had to get him to understand.

Dean's brows lifted. 'Does it worry you?' he asked.

Her eyes widened. 'Of course not,' she said. 'Why should it? It's nothing to do with me.'

'That's no answer,' Dean said bluntly. 'Would you believe me if I said that that was all in the past? Not quite as colourful as the Press would have you believe. Sure, I played around, but I'm no home-breaker. Those marriages were over before I arrived on the scene, and I'd like you to believe that. One thing I've learnt during all these years is that money, however necessary, attracts the more mendacious of the species, particularly the female. They were out for all they could get. It didn't bother me, but that was then, and this is now. Marriage was never considered, much to their fury. They paid me back in the only way open to them by citing me in the courts, hoping for some monetary consolation. Sometimes it worked, but not always.'

He caught Sheena's hand. 'I've only asked one woman to marry me, and that was my wife. Don't go away, Victoria, marry me,' he said quietly.

'Do you know what you're saying?' Sheena got out incredulously. She knew he was quite sober, but was he really in control of himself?

Dean gave her a wicked smile. 'Believe it or not, yes,' he said. 'I meant every word. I know it's come as a shock to you. But I want you to think about it, and I'm not letting you walk out of my life. Besides, think of the saving on the doctor's bills!'

Sheena shook her head, bewildered. 'I don't see—I can't——'

'Look, don't worry. We'll work something out, even if it means that you have to go on a few more tours. For the moment I'm content to leave things as they are, but only if you promise not to run out on me. For instance, Glenda's got a charity ball coming up at the end of the week, I'll make sure you're on the guest list. All you have to do is wander out into the garden around tennish. I'll see that Leroy is kept busy elsewhere.'

Sheena's head ached. Clandestine meetings in the garden, a marriage proposal; it was all a little

too much for her to cope with. She could only hope
that common sense would eventually win the day!

CHAPTER FOUR

DEAN dropped Sheena off outside the drive of Grasslands shortly before eleven p.m, too late, hopefully, for her grandmother still to be up, and too early to run into Brad.

This time she accepted the offer of a hot bedtime drink from Milly and took it to her bedroom, wondering if Milly had been given instructions to wait up for her. Knowing Gran, Sheena thought that was quite likely. If this was the case, Milly did not seem at all resentful, in fact she seemed to Sheena to be more approachable. Because she had dined with Leroy, and not her favourite? Anyway, it was a welcome change for Sheena, who had had enough aggro to contend with for one night.

She certainly had a lot to think about. After the first shock of Dean's proposal, and her natural reaction, she had to come to terms with the fact that he was serious.

It was a sad fact, she thought, that he had had to propose to the first woman he had met who was not a socialite and not out for gain. At least, that was the way Sheena saw it. She did not see that it was her charm and simple honesty not to mention the fact that she was a beauty in her own right, that had drawn Dean to her.

At this point her thoughts wandered to Brad Muldoon. A fine one he was to condemn Dean! He was no better himself, playing, as Dean had put it, with Glenda's feelings. All right, so Glenda deserved a setback, but that didn't excuse his part in the proceedings.

Sheena showered and got into bed. What on earth was she going to do? Dean had made it quite clear that he was not going to let her off the hook. He was going to continue to see her no matter what.

Now that he knew who she was, she couldn't feel safe or hide behind the fact that his threats to call on her had no substance as long as he did not have her address. She sighed. That hope had been a none-starter, had she but known it. It hadn't taken him long to place her, had it?

For a split second, she pondered on the advisability of owning up to their acquaintance. It was friendship and nothing else on her part anyway, and she rather thought that given time it would be the same for Dean, once he got over this crazy idea of wanting to marry her.

There seemed a spate of crazy ideas around this part of the globe, she thought sleepily. First Gran and now Dean, and she wondered vaguely if it was anything to do with the locality. On this thought, she fell asleep.

The following morning brought no enlightenment for Sheena, who was seriously considering sending that SOS to Mary. There used to be an old watchword that they had used in their youth when danger threatened, and all she had to do was to give the word to Mary. It meant ringing her, of course, she couldn't rely on the post, particularly as Gran would want to read any mail she received from home. Mary would be sure to ask what the trouble was.

Her step was heavy when she went down to breakfast, fully expecting a barrage of questions from Gran. Where had Leroy taken her to dinner? She would have to skate over that one, her saving grace being that she didn't know the area well enough to remember where the place was.

In the event however, she needn't have worried, for apart from a query of had she enjoyed herself, Gran seemed content to leave it at that. This caused a little concern to Sheena until she realised that Gran was still displeased with the association and did not mean to encourage it.

On the other hand, Brad, whom she would have expected to have something to say, even if it was only a sneering comment on her progress, was unusually silent, and Sheena wondered if Glenda had called his bluff and given him an ultimatum. Not that she could see him accepting it, but it did mean that they would both be crossed off the guest-list for the ball that Dean had said would be taking place on Saturday.

She didn't know why she was worrying, she told herself. Later, she would ring Mary from the hall telephone where she would get some privacy, and get her message across quite easily. The explaining could be done when she got home.

Sheena finished her breakfast in a state of calm composure, looking forward to getting back to normal again, and getting down to her studies.

Her peace of mind was not destined to last for long, for when she accompanied Gran to the lounge after breakfast, there was a letter lying on the hall table for her from Mary.

Her hopes of an early release from her troubles were dashed as she read Mary's cheerful communication. They were off to Sydney's Bondi Beach for a ten-day vacation.

As Sheena had expected, Gran wanted to read the letter for herself. 'Shaun will enjoy that,' she said. 'Mary's a fine girl, and I'm glad she's got a good husband. There aren't many who would welcome a younger brother into their home.'

Sheena tried hard to lighten her thoughts. She had been counting on Mary to get her out of her dilemma. Of all the times to go off to Sydney, she thought bitterly. 'Oh, Shaun and Don get on well,' she managed to reply. 'They've the same sense of humour, you know.'

Gran sighed as she took up her crochet. 'That's one thing that is missing these days where Brad's concerned,' she said. 'I've never known him so tetchy.'

Sheena gazed out of the french windows. 'You mean he does smile sometimes?' she asked, not really concentrating on the conversation, for her mind was still busy with her own problems.

Gran laid down her crochet. 'You know, you could be right,' she said, and there was somthing in her voice that caught Sheena's wandering attention and she looked back at her. 'I suppose I'm just living in a daydream,' Gran continued. 'You can't tell folk what to do, and what not to do. They have to make up their own minds. I'm as fond of that boy as I would be if he were my own child, but there's no arguing with the fact that he's been like a bear with a sore head since you came.'

Sheena blinked. Could this be her salvation? she wondered. 'So let me go home, Gran,' she said, hoping her eagerness did not show too much in her voice. 'Of course he's upset, and my being here makes it worse. Look, I'll pass my Finals and then arrange to come back for a holiday with you, how's that?'

Gran's brows furrowed. 'You've only just got here!' she said accusingly. 'That's not what I was getting at. I've decided to accept his friendship with Glenda Walling,' she announced grandly. 'If he wants to marry her, then I'll give them my blessing. I won't like it, but there are times when you have to give,' she ended firmly.

Sheena stayed silent. Either way, it didn't affect her, only from the point of view that Brad Muldoon would be relieved that his Gran had come to her senses where she and Brad were concerned. Not that there had been the slightest hope of any other conclusion, but the fact remained that she was not going to get the opportunity to leave.

At this point Brad joined them for a moment before going to work.

'I think it's about time I met your Glenda,' Gran announced, as he bent down to peck her cheek.

Sheena, although depressed, couldn't help feeling a spurt of amusement as she witnessed his reaction to this news, and the way those autocratic brows of his rose.

'Bring her to dinner this evening,' Gran commanded royally.

Brad stared at her for a moment before saying

bluntly, 'Not tonight, Gran. I've a late session at the office. Some other time, perhaps,' and left.

Gran watched the door close behind him, then looked at Sheena. 'What do you make of that?' she asked.

Sheena shook her head. 'Well, I suppose he has to break the news to Glenda first,' she said, adding with a hint of amusement in her voice, 'She'll need time to compose herself for the royal summons. You've a reputation of being hard to please, you know.'

'Stuff and nonsense!' Gran retorted. 'Take more than that to throw that girl out. Her father's money has given her open doors all over this state, and many more. No, there's more to it than that. If Brad had wanted to bring her to dinner he would have said so, wouldn't he? Late evening sessions don't last all that long, and he could have brought her over for a drink in the evening with us later, couldn't he?'

She was silent for a second or two, then chuckled. 'I've routed him, that's what I've done. Oh, he knew what I meant all right, and he's got to think about it.' She looked at Sheena. 'Is that how it ought to be?' she demanded. 'Time to think about it? Doesn't sound right to me.' There was a satisfactory note in her voice and she settled down to her crochet.

Mary's letter was not the only communication Sheena received that day, for there was a telephone call for her later that morning from Leroy.

'I can't take you out this week, Sheena,' he said. 'I've a rotten boil on my face. It's been agony. Doc said he couldn't do anything until it comes to a head, and I'm certainly not going out looking like this.

I'd be the laughing-stock of the place. It's on the end
of my nose. I don't mind you seeing me, I'm sure
you wouldn't laugh at me. Do you think you could
call over to see me? I'm getting bored to tears on my
own. Mother's visiting her sister in Auckland, thank
goodness. The last time I had a spate of these things,
she dosed me with all sorts of rotten medicines, and
at least I'm spared that.'

Sheena didn't have to think long about it. It
would get her out of Grasslands for a while, and she
needed something to keep herself occupied, even if it
was only listening to Leroy's moans. She wouldn't
have to stay long. 'Very well. Is there anything you
want brought in for you? Magazines, papers?' she
asked.

A delighted Leroy mentioned a couple of
magazines that he would like her to get for him, and
then gave her his address. 'Take a taxi,' he told her,
'and put it on our account. Mother uses them for
everything.' He gave her the name of the firm to
call, adding, 'Get the driver to stop at the newsagent
just before you turn off into our avenue. He'll
probably know which one I mean. You'll stay to
lunch, won't you?'

Sheena wasn't so sure about that, but if he was on
his own, she might prepare something for him, she
thought, as she went back to the lounge to tell Gran
the news.

After a few grumbles, Gran accepted the fact that
Sheena was off on a ministering-angel act. 'But
don't let him monopolise you,' she warned her. 'If it
were anyone else but Leroy, I would have second
thoughts about your going to his place. As it is, I've

no worries on that score; they've enough staff to look after a place twice that size.'

After promising to be back for dinner, hopefully before that, Sheena thought, she slipped away to her room to collect her bag and a light cardigan, and then rang the taxi firm Leroy had given her and in a very short time was on her way.

Sheena first ensured that the cabby would accept the fact that the trip to Leroy's home was to go on their account. It didn't matter if he didn't. She had enough to pay for the journey, but it would save her some embarrassment at the end of the journey.

Going by the preferential treatment she received after she had made this tentative enquiry, Sheena presumed that Leroy's mother must be the best customer the firm had on their books. Had it been winter, she was sure that a rug would have been produced to stave off the cold. When she recalled Leroy's taste in cars it was not at all surprising that his mother preferred this mode of transport to his open two-seater.

The journey took twenty minutes, including the stop at the newsagents, and Sheena saw more of Canberra, and marvelled at the open spaces, the countless trees, parkland, and brilliant flower displays that were at their best in the spring. It was the right time to be there, she thought, and on the whole she preferred it to Melbourne's dignified atmosphere, with its settled-in citizenship with their beautiful houses, happy to echo old colonial ties with the past.

But Canberra, she thought, spoke of the future, not of the past, and that in itself was exciting.

There would always be work for a variety of professions, not only for those involved in the running of the country, but for the services required to keep the administration ticking over smoothly. At this point Brad Muldoon came to mind, and she hastily turned her thoughts to other channels. Whatever his work, it was no concern of hers, as he himself would take great pleasure in informing her.

Leroy's home was not unlike Grasslands, in that it was more of a villa than a house, set in its own grounds well screened from idle curiosity.

Sheena had no sooner got to the front door than it was whisked open by Leroy. The tip of his nose was covered by a dressing held in place by a strip of plaster.

It had to be said that in spite of Leroy's assurance that Sheena would not laugh at him, she did not find it easy to hide her first highly amused reaction to his appearance. Leroy's nose was his most prominent feature.

With a quick, almost furtive action, he ushered her in, and led the way to a room that was obviously a lounge. After her first difficult moments of having to compose her expression and not let Leroy down by letting her sense of humour get the better of her, the room she found herself in immediately quenched all other thought.

The dominant colour was purple with lilac undertones: purple velvet furnishings on the upholstery, violet-coloured walls, rich purple curtaining, and a deep purple and violet carpeting with mahogany furniture inlaid with gold filigree patterning.

'Awful, isn't it?' Leroy said. 'Mother's idea of splendour, you know,' he ended lamely.

Sheena could now see what Brad had been getting at when he warned her about Leroy's mother, and her hopes for her son. Nothing short of royalty, she thought, would fit into this décor.

'You've got my magazines,' Leroy exclaimed happily, as she handed them to him, and gestured to one of the plush armchairs. 'You can sit on them,' he said with a wry smile. 'In fact, they're quite comfortable.'

Sheena sat but it didn't seem right somehow. She felt that she ought to be dressed for the occasion, liking wearing a crinoline instead of jeans and blouse. She could almost sense the outrage Leroy's mother would have felt had she been present.

They took lunch in an equally ornate dining-room, whose large proportions were emphasised by mirrored walls, making Sheena feel she was in an aquarium. They were served by a morose man who gave her the impression that his thoughts were the same as his employer's on the subject of wearing the correct dress for such an auspicious occasion.

Shortly after lunch, Sheena was able to get away, but not without the promise of another visit the following day.

All in all, Sheena thought, as the taxi took her back to Grasslands, she felt very sorry for Leroy, who would probably end up marrying a paler caricature of his mother. From then on it would be open war between the women, as to who could wield the stronger power over the poor man.

To both Sheena and Gran's surprise, Brad joined them in the lounge later that evening, and provided

Sheena with a sherry when he got himself a drink.
This action caused Sheena a little worry, as she
wondered if he had found out about her association
with Dean, and was softening her up before throwing her to the wolves.

'Glenda rang through today,' he said, as he
settled himself in an easy chair, his long legs streched
out in front of him. 'Invited us to a charity ball on
Saturday,' he remarked, looking at Sheena. 'I
thought it was very kind of her to have remembered
you.'

Sheena gave him a wary look. She didn't care for
the sudden turn in his approach to her, but said
nothing, just nodded. Dean had obviously got his
way, and got her invited.

Gran looked pleased. 'Very civil of her,' she said,
and at Brad's suspicious look towards her, went on,
'It's time they got acquainted. We'll have to get you
a ballgown.'

As Sheena hadn't anything approaching a ballgown, she had to accept the offer, but did not miss
Brad's curled lips and guessed his thoughts. On the
scrounge again, and wasn't she doing well by her
relations? The small incident helped put her mind at
rest. This was more like the man she had come to
know, and he had reverted to form.

She was relieved on another point too. He didn't
know about Dean, couldn't have done. He wasn't
likely to miss a chance of sneering at her attempts to
get herself a rich husband, or lowering her stock in
front of Gran, particularly after Gran's assertion
that Sheena was not looking for a millionaire.

'According to Glenda,' Brad went on, oblivious of

Sheena's uncomplimentary thoughts, 'her father looks like settling down at last, and is talking of marriage. She doesn't know who the woman is, only that her name's Victoria.'

At this point, Sheena, who had been taking a sip of her sherry, suddenly choked and ended up in a spasm of coughing.

Brad gave her a cold look. 'I presume the name has amused you. It's old-fashioned, I'll admit, but to me it sounds eminently respectable, and the type of woman to straighten him out.'

Gran's 'Hmph!' showed her feelings in the matter, but not wanting to cause a rift between them, she changed the conversation by asking him how things had gone at the office.

Sheena didn't really remember anything at all about the rest of the conversation. Gran wasn't the only one in for a shock if the truth ever came out. Brad Muldoon was in line for a much greater one. His words 'eminently respectable' kept coming to mind, as she tried to look interested in other subjects. As soon as she could she pleaded tiredness and went to bed.

CHAPTER FIVE

SHEENA paid another visit to Leroy the next day. Having given her word, she was duty-bound to keep it.

This time she had to listen to him bemoaning the fact that he couldn't attend the ball, the invitation for which had arrived that morning. 'I knew about it, of course,' he said, 'but there's so much going on that we have to get these reminders. I suppose you've been invited?' he asked Sheena, who nodded. 'Well, there you are, and I can't take you,' he groaned. 'I shall have to give an excuse, I suppose. There are a lot of summer colds around just now, and that's what I'll have to have,' he ended miserably.

Sheena did her best to try and cheer him up, but as she wasn't too happy herself, it was hard going, and she was relieved when she was able to take her leave soon after lunch.

Eventually it was Saturday, and Sheena, dressed in the gown her grandmother had ordered for her, a pale green floating creation that brought out the green in her eyes, and looking like a fashion plate, was driven to the ball in Brad's car. She would have preferred a taxi, but her grandmother gave her no choice in the matter by asking Brad to take her.

As before the conversation on the journey did nothing to add to her expectancy of enjoying the evening. After a back-handed compliment on her appearance, thanks to her grandmother's generosity, he silkily enquired after Leroy, and his failure to convey her to the ball, in a manner that suggested there was more to this than met the eye.

A furious Sheena quickly disputed this. 'He's got a chill,' she said frostily.

Brad gave her a sideways look. 'So he says,' he said. 'It's a useful excuse, any way,' he added sneeringly. 'If you ask me, his mother's got wind of the association and is taking no chances. You'll have to look elsewhere for your rich benefactor, but I don't think you'll have any luck around here,' he added pithily.

Sheena's hands clenched into small fists, and she gritted her teeth. How she longed to tell him that he needn't worry on her account, she had already found her rich suitor. The temptation was very great, but somehow she resisted it, for Gran's sake more than his. She didn't care two hoots about him, but she did care about Gran.

When they walked into the large ballroom, and located their hostess, Sheena found herself once more on the receiving end of a very cool stare from Glenda Walling, as she stood beside the tall, handsome, tuxedoed figure of Brad, and had to thank her nicely for the invitation, for which she received an off-hand 'Oh, any relative of Brad's is welcome,' reply, but the look in her pale blue eyes did not echo this sentiment, and Sheena was pleased to be able to move away from them and mix with the company.

Her fears of finding herself out on a limb were

dispelled by a small group of young men with a keen
eye for a presentable female, and she was soon
engulfed with partners for whatever dance-tune was
played.

The absence of Leroy undoubtedly made all the
difference, and an out-of breath Sheena, begging off
a third dance in succession, actually began to wish
that he was present.

Several times during that evening, she caught
Brad's eyes on her, obviously checking up on her
behaviour and her dancing partner. His scowl
denoted his annoyance that she seemed to be
enjoying herself.

Around nine-thirty, she saw Dean. He was
standing by the french windows, and he too had a
scowl on his face, and she was a bit dismayed when
he came over to her corner and requested a dance
with her.

Her quick surreptitious glance around the room to
see where Brad was, and if he had seen Dean
approach her, was answered by Deans's casual,
'Don't worry, Glenda's taken him to see the new
fountain we've just had installed in the patio,' as he
led her on to the floor.

Sheena could only hope that Glenda managed to
spin out their absence until Dean whisked her off
from the company, for that was what he had come
for, she was certain. Sure enough, half-way through
the dance he caught her hand and led her through a
door along what seemed to be the main section of the
house, and to the rear, where he halted before a side
door, and ushered her into what was obviously a
study.

'Another bolt-hole of mine,' he said with a smile. 'We will not be disturbed here,' he added, as he tightened his hold on Sheena's hand. 'You look beaut,' he said quietly, and would have kissed her, had Sheena not drawn back to avoid any such action. For a moment his hard features tightened, then he shrugged lightly. 'Rushing my fences, I'm afraid,' he said, 'It wasn't easy watching you being surrounded by other men, all wanting to dance with you. Have you thought about my proposal?' he added suddenly

Sheena disengaged her hand from his. 'Let's put it this way,' she said, managing to keep her voice light. 'I'm still recovering from the shock.'

With that, Dean had to be content. The rest of the evening was spent in Sheena's trying to extract a promise from him to leave things as they were. He was by no means entirely agreeable to this arrangement, and threatened dire consequences that were only forestalled by Sheena's warning him that she would not see him at all should he go ahead.

Dean returned Sheena to the ballroom around one o'clock, taking her round the rear garden and back to the french windows, to give her the excuse of taking a stroll in the gardens should anyone be interested in her movements.

It was as well for Sheena that this precaution had been taken, for the minute she stepped back into the ballroom, Brad pounced on her. 'Where the devil have you been?' he demanded angrily. 'You've been missing well over an hour.' He stared behind her, looking, Sheena surmised, for the companion of her nocturnal wandering.

'It was hot in here,' Sheena replied calmly. 'So I went for a stroll in the gardens.'

'For an hour?' Brad sneered disbelievingly.

Actually, it was more than an hour, but Sheena kept this to herself. 'We only have small hops at home,' she said, trying hard to sound apologetic. 'This is all a bit much for me.'

'Out of your depth, are you? Well, I thought you would be, but there's no convincing Gran. She'll keep on pushing you up the social scale. You'll just have to stand up to her,' he advised her sourly.

'I've tried that,' Sheena said, 'but it doesn't seem to make any difference, and the last time I tried to get out of a do, you didn't co-operate. Perhaps next time you'll come out on my side,' she added coldly.

'You bet!' Brad replied grimly, then seeing Glenda heading their way, turned back to Sheena. 'Don't go wandering out again, do you hear? The ball ends in half an hour, and I don't want to have to go out looking for you. Is that clear?' He then left her to join Glenda.

It was about a quarter to two before they got away, with an irate Sheena sick of being treated like a third-class citizen by Brad Muldoon. She hadn't even been allowed to take her leave of her hostess. Not that that bothered her, but she was annoyed when Brad had barged in on a conversation she was having with a rather persistent man who demanded her address and phone number. She was in the middle of explaining that she was only on a visit to Canberra when her arm was seized and she was hustled out of the hall, into the driveway and towards his car.

'That was unforgivable!' she said to Brad, as he hustled her into his car, seated himself, and switched on the ignition. 'I was just explaining to that gentleman that I was——'

'That was no gentleman,' Brad growled, as he steered the car out of the driveway. 'And I sincerely hope that he was not the one who accompanied you on your evening walk. That's another thing Gran didn't take into account, and she expects me to act as nursemaid to a country cousin. It's not on, no way!'

'Don't worry,' Sheena said between her teeth. 'This is positively the last time I go anywhere in your company.' She turned away from him, and stared out of the window, trying to distance herself as far as possible from him in spite of the confined car space.

A few minutes later, Brad swore under his breath, and Sheena held herself in readiness for hearing what else she had done to upset him. There was no telling with him.

'I forgot to put a spare can of petrol in the car,' he said; 'I was so damned angry at finding myself lumbered with you, everything else went out of my mind.'

'Thank you, Sheena replied icily. 'I knew it would have to be my fault.'

At this point the car stuttered to a stop, and Brad's fingers beat an angry tattoo on the wheel. 'Not even enough to get us to a station,' he muttered furiously,' and the nearest is a good two miles away.'

Sheena settled herself more firmly in her seat. So he would have to tramp two miles for petrol. Good! She couldn't have wished it on a nicer person!

Brad opened his door. 'Come on, then,' he ordered as he began to get out of the car.

Sheena stared back at him through the faint light of the dashboard. 'I'm not going anywhere!' she stated firmly.

'Oh, yes, you are,' he said grimly. 'I'm not leaving you alone at this time of day, so get marching'

'You can lock the car, can't you?' Sheena said. 'No one will bother at this time of the morning. I shall be perfectly safe.'

'Locking the car's not much use when it comes to a determined thief, they've got duplicates, and I'm not arguing with you. Get!' In spite of the fact that it had been a warm day, the early-morning air was definitely on the chilly side. Sheena was glad of the fur stole that her grandmother had lent her, and she pulled it tightly around her shoulders as she stood shivering beside the car.

They had gone only a few steps when Sheena realised that her comfortable dancing shoes with their, high pointed heels were not ideal for a route-march, especially as she was trying to keep pace with Brad's long, athletic strides.

'For goodness' sake!' he exploded, as she complained that he was going too fast. 'It's those stupid shoes you're wearing. Take them off, or we'll be here all morning, and I've a job to go to, in case you've forgotten. We can't all be lounge-lizards.'

Sheena looked down at the section of the road they were on, lit by the eerie glow of an orange street-light. She didn't fancy walking in her stockinged feet, but there was no other solution, so she quickly

slipped them off, and ran to catch up with the tall
form of Brad now some way in front of her.

Once or twice she winced as small flints sprayed
on to the pathway from passing cars and stabbed her
feet. As her discomfort grew, so did her hate for
Brad Muldoon.

The first few drops of rain were felt after they had
gone a few hundred yards, and halted Brad in his
stride. 'Damn. That's all we need,' he exploded,
and glared at Sheena. 'If it weren't for you I'd go
on. A bit of rain never hurt anyone, but it would just
be my luck for you to catch pneumonia, especially in
that flimsy get-up. If it weren't for Gran I'd risk it,
but as it is——' He turned back abruptly, and a
relieved Sheena followed him back to the car.

When they were settled back in the car, Sheena
had one last try at getting him to leave her and go to
collect some petrol. 'You might come across a phone
booth,' she said,' then you could get them to send
someone out with some.'

Brad gave her a look that she sensed rather than
saw, and it wasn't very complimentary. 'At this time
of morning,' he said with heavy emphasis, 'there are
no staff around to answer the call. The pumps are
automatic, or hadn't you realised that? Before you
make any more useless suggestions like ringing a
friend to oblige, forget it! I'm not likely to advertise
the fact that I was fool enough to forget to check up
on my tank. Quite apart from that, I can't leave you
here on your own. You're quite safe with me, but
others might not be so fussy.'

Sheena had had enough. She didn't care about
anything now, except putting this arrogant brute in

his place, no matter what it cost her. 'Really,' she
said, managing to keep her voice calm, and that was
a feat in itself, 'I do think you ought to show a little
more respect for your Glenda's future stepmother,
and if you do decide to marry her, your mother-in-
law.

There was a stupefied silence on Brad's part for a
second, then, 'What did you say?'

'I believe you heard me,' Sheena said, feeling a
glow of triumph filter through her cold body. She
would marry Dean, she thought. A girl could do
worse, and she believed that they would deal very
nicely together. Who knows, in time she would come
to love him, even if it were only for protecting her
from this man's constant sneers and lowering
comments.

'You're making it up,' Brad accused her. 'That's
a fairy-story if ever I heard one. Dean Walling's
never met you. He wasn't at the garden party I took
you to, and as far as I know he didn't put in an
appearance at the ball, so pull the other leg!'

Sheena sighed. 'He was, you know. He was there
on both occasions. I first met him at the garden
party.' She went on to relate how she had come to
meet him, and had met him twice since then, ending
with 'He asked me to marry him, and I've decided
to accept his offer. As you so pointedly remarked
earlier this evening, rich benefactors aren't that easy
to find.'

'I don't believe you,' Brad said flatly. 'How come
Gran doesn't know about this grand passion of
yours?'

Sheena drew the fur cape closer around her. 'How

could I tell her?' she said angrily. 'Dean knows how things are. That's why nothing was said before, because we didn't want her to find out. Now she'll have to know, and I shall have to tell her.'

There was something in her voice that got through to Brad who stared back at her. 'So it's true, then?' he asked, and her silence verified it. 'So,' he said furiously, 'that's who you were with this evening while I was looking for you and wondering where the devil you were. You were canoodling with Walling in his private quarters.'

Sheena highly resented the way he had described her meeting with Dean, making it sound like an illicit amorous assignation. 'It wasn't like that at all!' she replied indignantly. 'If you must know, I spent most of the time trying to persuade him to keep our association quiet. I needn't have bothered, as it happens.'

'And how are you going to put it to Gran?' he asked silkily.

Sheena started at him. 'Put what to Gran?' she asked, not quite catching his meaning.

'Oh, just the fact that you have decided to marry a man you've only just met. I do hope you're not going to tell her that you love him, or any other sentimental rubbish.'

Sheena drew herself up from her lounging position. 'I shall tell her that I respect him.'

Brad's harsh laugh cut off the rest of the sentence. 'Of course you do. You'd respect anyone with a bank balance like his, wouldn't you? You'd have jumped at the chance of taking me, only I nipped that little scheme in the bud, didn't I?'

Sheena's erect form stiffened at this very unfair charge. 'I wouldn't take you at any price!' she declared furiously.

'Easy to say,' Brad scoffed, 'now that you think that you've got Dean Walling in the bag. It would be a different story if I made a dead set at you, I can promise you.'

Sheena had no premonition of what was about to happen. If she had thought about it, she would have come to the conclusion that he was about to reach into the small compartment on the dashboard in front of her, perhaps for a torch, so she was astounded when she found herself being forcibly pulled into his arms, her indignant response being smothered by a bruising kiss that went on and on until she was gasping for breath.

It seemed an eternity before he let her go, and his soft, insinuating, 'See what I mean,' was the last straw for Sheena shaken as she was.

'Don't you ever touch me again!' she managed to get out, rubbing her hand over her mouth still stinging from his punishment. Somewhere along the way, she had touched him on a raw spot. Because she hadn't appreciated his manliness? He had obviously expected her to go under and weakly acknowledge his mastery. 'You can save that kind of demonstration for those who appreciate it. You're wasting your time with me.'

'In that case, we'll try again, shall we, and see if I can get it right,' he said, as he reached out for her again.

There was no telling what would have happened then if a patrol car hadn't stopped beside them, and a nice young patrolman had politely enquired what they were doing parked on a main road at that time of the morning.

A furious Brad had had to explain the position, which sounded highly unlikely even to Sheena, even though she knew that it was the truth. After obliging them with enough petrol to get them home, he took off with a salute, and a sly smile that suggested that he'd seen it all before and that they should have picked a more remote spot for a cuddle.

'I only hope he didn't recognise me,' Brad growled, as he switched on the ignition with a vicious action that showed his feelings. 'It'll be all round Parliament House tomorrow if he did.'

'Oh, what a shame!' Sheena said, and try as she might she couldn't help finding the situation comic. He was such a pillar of respectability, and wouldn't it be terrible if he landed up with a reputation like Dean's? The more she thought about it, the funnier it seemed, and she went into a fit of giggles.

'If you don't stop this minute, I'll park at the nearest lay-by and strangle the life out of you,' Brad growled menacingly.

Sheena swallowed. 'I'm sorry,' she said, wiping her streaming eyes, and making a tremendous effort to control herself. 'It's just that—oh, dear,' and she was off again.

Happily for Sheena, they were nearing home, so she was able to return in one piece, but Brad's quiet 'I haven't finished with you yet' warning before she rushed into the house left her sober, and rather worried about what he was going to say to Gran before she had had time to explain things to her.

CHAPTER SIX

ALTHOUGH it was Sunday, Sheena went down to breakfast a little earlier than was necessary. She was haunted by the worry that Brad would seize the first opportunity of getting a word in with Gran. No doubt he would dwell on the sly behaviour of the girl she had welcomed into her home as one of her kin, and would take great delight in informing her that she had taken a viper to her bosom.

Gran, as Sheena knew, was an early riser, and was already in the lounge when she got down. Her first apprehensive glance towards her told her that as yet she had had no startling exposures thrown at her. Her interested query, 'Did you enjoy the ball?' proved this.

Sheena felt that she hadn't much time to get it all off her chest, for Brad might walk in at any moment and she would lose her chance, but Gran's next words dispelled this fear. As Sheena gave an abrupt nod to her query, she went on, 'Brad left early. He's going for an early-morning ride, with you know who. I don't expect we'll be seeing much of him today.'

Inwardly, Sheena felt a wave of relief wash over her, but it didn't alter the fact that she had to come clean about her association with Dean, and only hope that his assessment of Gran's character proved right.

Taking a deep breath, she plunged in, telling Gran everything, and carefully watching the bright, startled look that came into her eyes as she related the story. She ended with, 'I'm sorry I didn't tell you before, but I knew how much you disliked him, and didn't want to hurt you.'

Gran sat silent for a moment or two, then asked quietly, 'Why are you telling me now? You said he was perfectly agreeable to keeping your association quiet.'

Sheena looked away from those enquiring eyes of hers, and gave a slight shrug. 'I had to, I'm sorry to say. You see I told Brad last night.'

Gran's eyebrows rose a fraction higher. 'Now why was that?' she asked.

Sheena gave a deep sigh. 'Well, you know how he is,' she said. 'Whatever goes wrong, it's my fault. He ran out of petrol on the way home, and it's a thing he never does, which I can well believe. He blamed it on me, said he was so mad at being lumbered with me that it put everything else out of his mind. Then he was on about Leroy, and wasn't it funny that he couldn't take me to the ball, and hinting that his mother had decided that I wasn't quite the girl she wanted her son to get involved with. Oh, you know what he's like, perfectly beastly. So I just let him have it. Told him that he ought to be a little more polite to someone who would be his mother-in-law if he married Glenda.'

There was a long silence after this somewhat bald statement, and Sheena glanced apprehensively towards her grandmother. With wide eyes she saw the silent shaking of her frail shoulders, and thought for one awful second that she was about to have a stroke. Suddenly she realised that Gran's paroxysms were caused by laughter, deep hearty laughter that filled her being, and when at last she was able to catch her breath, she said, 'I only wish I could have been there to see his face.'

Sheena caught her mood and started chuckling, too. 'I'm afraid I was too angry at the time really to appreciate that side of it, but I did have to smile when the patrolman came to our rescue.' She went on to tell Gran of that and Brad's furious comment afterwards, much to the old lady's amusement.'

'Oh, dear,' gasped Gran, wiping her streaming eyes. 'Never a dull moment, but it won't do him any harm, you know. As I said, I don't know what's got into him lately. There was a time when he would have seen the funny side of things, too.' She shook her head, and then sobered abruptly. 'Did Dean Walling really mean it when he asked you to marry him?' she asked.

Sheena sobered too, and stared down at her hands.' I believe he does,' she replied. 'That's the maddest part of it all, Gran. I mean, he hardly knows me, we've only met three times. It doesn't seem conceivable that he's serious, but I'm sure he is.'

'And you?' Gran asked.

Sheena looked back at her. 'I like him, Gran. He's not at all the kind of person they write about in the papers. I mean, I'm not saying he's a saint. He isn't, but then no one is. He lost his wife when Glenda was quite young, and he says he's never asked anyone to marry him until now. I believe him. I suppose in time, I might——' her voice trailed off.

Gran patted her hand. 'Well, at least you're being sensible about it, and not letting it go to your head, which is what I expected of you. I think I should like to meet this man.'

Sheena gaped at her, then quickly recovered. 'Why, you old fraud!' she exclaimed softly. 'You're not a bit shocked, are you? And I was so worried about telling you.'

Gran gave a sniff. 'I've had to come to terms with Brad and this Glenda, and that wasn't easy, so I might as well go the whole hog. I shall invite both of them to dinner on Wednesday evening,' she declared, and sat back, looking hugely pleased with herself.

Sheena was completely nonplussed. Dean would be delighted, she knew, and she wished she could say the same for herself and Brad, who would hit the roof, she was sure. He didn't like arrangements being made without his say-so. See how he had side-stepped Gran's earlier invitation to him to bring Glenda to dinner.

Gran's earlier assumption that Brad would be off the scene for the rest of the day proved wrong when he walked in to breakfast shortly after they had begun theirs, and Milly dashed out to prepare his.

'I thought you'd be having breakfast with Glenda,' Gran said.

'Who said that I was with Glenda?' Brad queried, with a lift of his autocratic eyebrows as he sat down, Then he glared across at Sheena. 'Told Gran your news yet?' he asked silkily.

Sheena's head went up and her small chin stuck out. 'Yes, I have,' she replied.

Brad took a sip of his coffee, and his eyes were on

his grandmother. 'So?' he asked.

Gran's faded blue eyes met his. 'Yes, I was surprised, but as I now realise, you can't tell folk what to do. It's up to them,' she said placidly.

Brad stared at her. 'You mean you don't object?' he demanded. 'Thinks he wants to marry her, has she told you that?'

Gran nodded. 'She's told me everything,' she replied calmly.

Her equanimity infuriated Brad. 'And you believe her? Well, it's more than I do! I seem to recall Glenda mentioning someone called Victoria.' He looked at Sheena. 'I don't recall that being your name,' he added sneeringly.

'As a matter of fact, it's what Dean calls me, because I come from Victoria. But I don't have to prove anything to you,' Sheena replied angrily.

'That's right, you know, Brad,' Gran said, her eyes beginning to twinkle with a secret inward thought. 'We'll soon know, anyway. I'm inviting Mr Walling, and Glenda, if she'd like to come, to dinner on Wednesday evening.'

'You're what!' thundered Brad.

'There is no need to shout, Brad Muldoon,' Gran said, with dignity. 'I want to meet him, and of course, Glenda, too, but that's up to you. I thought it would only be polite to invite them both, but you don't have to be present if you'd rather go off somewhere by yourselves.'

'Do you know what kind of a man he is?' Brad snarled. 'He's had more affairs than I've had hot meals. Is that the kind of man you want a relation of ours to marry?'

'Nice of you to include me in the family,' Sheena said in a tight voice. 'You seem to forget that I'm a distant cousin, and nothing else.'

'You're a Muldoon!' Brad shouted at her. 'And we expect some consideration of that fact, money or no money. If you don't give Walling his marching orders, I will!' Totally ignoring the fact that Milly had just entered with his breakfast, he stormed out of the room.

Gran's amused eyes met the angry ones of Sheena, who flung down her napkin, and said exasperatedly, 'It's not funny, Gran. I don't think you ought to go through with that invitation.'

'I most certainly will,' Gran said firmly. 'I have a right to meet the man who wants to marry you. If he's up to no good, then there's no surer way of calling his bluff, is there? Brad will just have to put up with it. He's had things all his own way for far too long, with silly women falling all over him. It will do him a power of good to find that he's not the only attraction around.'

Sheena heartily agreed with this sentiment, particularly as she recalled the previous evening when he had lowered his standards in an attempt to prove to himself, and to her, his superiority when it came to physical attractions. Yet she could see nothing but trouble ahead, should Dean accept the invitation. She was sure he would.

Gradually the time slipped by to Wednesday, and Sheena, who had been trying to keep herself occupied, was actually glad of the visits paid to Leroy, if only to take her mind off the coming dinner party. Dean had accepted, as she had known he would, and Glenda, too, apparently, as Brad had told them surlily, adding icily that he had had no choice in the matter. It all added up to a perfectly ghastly evening in store.

By now, Leroy's isolation was almost at an end, and he was about to re-emerge into society, full of plans for Sheena's future. From these she had to extricate herself without hurting his feelings. Eventually, he would hear about her friendship with Dean, and there was nothing she could do about that. Her conscience was clear; she had not encouraged him to look upon her as anything other than a friend.

That had been something else that had infuriated Brad, who had eventually found out why Leroy had been missing from the scene. The news had been given to him by Gran, for Sheena had made no mention of it, and his sneering comment of, 'Playing the ministering angel again, eh?' was the only intimation that he knew about it. It was also a sly allusion to her meeting with Dean, and she was well aware of it.

The only person, apart perhaps from Dean and Glenda, who was actually looking forward to the dinner party was Gran, who seemed to take on a new lease of life. She fussed about the meal and insisted that they dressed for the occasion. She told Sheena in a conspiratorial manner that she had given Stanley the evening off. 'He knows, of course, who we're having to dinner,' she said, 'but he's coming to terms with the fact that you can't change things by wishful thinking.'

This was a great pity, Sheena thought ironically,

as she had indulged in some wishful thinking of her own. Her wish that she could go home and get on with her life was uppermost in her mind!

Once again, Gran had played fairy godmother over Sheena's clothes, and Sheena found several garments laid out on her bed, including two day suits and two cocktail dresses. It made Sheena want to weep. She knew it was of no use protesting to Gran, or even trying to thank her for her generosity, for she had made it quite clear that such sentiments were unwelcome to her. It was her pleasure, she had said, to provide for Sheena. This was all very well, but Sheena couldn't help feeling a little like Cinderella in the outfits, complete with one of the ugly sisters or in her case an ugly brother. He seemed determined to ruin things for her.

For the dinner party she wore one of the cocktail dresses, three-quarter length, of a soft peach colour, with tracings of gold leaves entwined round the mandarin-styled collar.

Prompt at seven-thirty, Dean and Glenda arrived, to be greeted by a stiff and very erect Brad. They were taken in to meet his grandmother, and a very nervous Sheena stood beside her.

Gran looked resplendent in a black velvet evening dress complete with a triple row of pearls, and formidable enough to impress even Dean, who bent forward and kissed her frail outstretched hand with an old-world courtesy that certainly went a long way towards lulling her earlier suspicions of his character. To this scene Brad gave a hardly disguised sneer, which happily was missed by all except Sheena. She quickly looked away and concentrated on Dean and Glenda.

When the formal introductions were over, and before any other conversation could be started, Dean took the initiative by catching hold of Sheena's hand and saying to Glenda, 'This is my Victoria.'

Glenda stared at Sheena who felt herself grow pink with embarrassment. 'But how——' Glenda began bewilderedly.

Dean laughed, and told her the story of their meeting. 'If one can die of panic, then I'd have gone then,' he added sombrely, although the look in his eyes belied this statement. 'Victoria's cool hands saved my life,' he went on.

'Stuff and nonsense!' Sheena broke in indignantly, unwittingly echoing Gran's favourite saying. 'Don't believe him. The truth of the matter was that he'd taken a hard ride after a heavy meal.'

Glenda's giggle was cut off by Brad's growled, 'Hmph!' as if to say any fool could have reassured him on that point. Gran's sharp look of rebuke at him forestalled any attempt on his part actually to say so.

The dinner proved the most awkward time for Sheena, with Brad glowering not only at her but at Dean as well. Glenda grew chummier as time went on. Now that her fears where Brad and Sheena were concerned were laid to rest, she positively oozed charm, but Sheena rather preferred the way she had been treated before. An off-hand Glenda was easier to deal with than an effusive one.

Invitations were given to this and that function, and of course Sheena had to attend a dinner party

Glenda was giving that Friday evening. Glenda made the mistake of appealing to Brad to attend as well, and she was surprised by his cold reply that he would be tied up that evening.

Sheena had also noted the way Dean had been studying Brad. He must have been aware of the antagonism directed towards him, and that seemed to afford him some amusement.

After dinner, Gran, Sheena and Dean settled in the lounge for what Sheena suspected would be an interrogation of Dean by Gran. Brad and Glenda took a stroll in the gardens, and for the first time that evening Sheena was able to relax.

Needless to say, Dean charmed his way into Gran's good books simply by being himself, and soon they were chatting like old friends.

This state of harmony however was not destined to last for long. As soon as Brad and Glenda came in from their stroll it was obvious that they had been quarrelling. Glenda's high colour and Brad's set lips confirmed this without Glenda's angry, 'I think it's time we left, Father. I have the start of a head-ache.'

This time it was Dean who showed his displeasure, but he directed it at Brad with a smooth 'Had an argument?'

'Just a difference of opinion,' Brad replied stiffly, a reply that made Glenda toss her head and tap an elegant shoe to show that she was by no means placated.

Dean was forced to agree to his daughter's wishes, and rose to the occasion. He issued an invitation to Gran and Sheena to dine with him on Sunday, reminding Sheena that he would see her anyway on the Friday evening and would collect her at eight.

At this point, Brad's smooth,' There's no need to put yourself out. I shall bring Sheena with me,' surprised everybody, not least Glenda who was under the impression that he had turned the invitation down. He had, Sheena recalled.

Dean had not liked this at all, but could hardly say so, particularly as Glenda had perked up at the news and gave an abrupt nod of acceptance.

Dean's feelings were echoed by Sheena, who was absolutely furious with Brad. She would have preferred to be taken by Dean, and angrily said so when they were alone. Gran had gone to bed immediately after Dean and Glenda had left, stating that it was past her bedtime.

'I don't want you to take me to that dinner,' Sheena said abruptly. 'I thought you said that you were tied up for that evening. Why did you change your mind?'

Brad studied her through half closed lids. 'Because I intend to keep an eye on you, that's why,' he replied harshly. 'Gran's like all the other women, mesmerised by the fellow. I thought she had more sense, so it's up to me to watch over you.'

Sheena was so angry she had trouble getting her breath, but she was determined to let him know she didn't intend him to have any say in her affairs. 'I like Dean,' she got out, 'and if anyone has to be watched, it's you! As far as I'm concerned Dean has acted the perfect gentleman, and that's more than can be said for you. What do you think Glenda would say if she knew that you had forced your attentions on me?'

Brad's wicked grin caught Sheena by surprise, and his languid, 'A little competition does no harm,' made her catch her breath.

'You don't care for Glenda at all, do you?' she flung at him. 'Just amusing yourself, aren't you? And you have the nerve to criticise Dean. Well, let me tell you something. Dean isn't fooled by you. He was pretty sure that you weren't serious about Glenda.'

Brad's eyes narrowed a fraction more. 'Told you that, did he?' he said. 'You did get chummy, didn't you? Well, it takes one to recognise one. He's had enough practice to be able to judge, I'll say that for him. For your information Glenda has a lot of her father in her. She's only interested in me because she can't twist me round her little finger, and she's not used to that. I have a little more sense than to go overboard for a woman like that. Does that answer your question?'

Sheena's eyes flashed. 'It's nothing to do with me,' she replied coldly, 'only the fact that you have no right to run Dean down. People in glass houses shouldn't throw stones.'

'And little girls on the lookout for a rich husband shouldn't bite the hand that feeds them,' Brad said softly, as he moved towards her. 'We've some unfinished business, you and I, haven't we?'

Sheena's eyes widened as she caught his meaning, and backed away from that purposeful look in his eyes. 'Oh, no, you don't,' she said hastily. 'You're not working out your frustrated ego on me.'

'Afraid, are you?' Brad taunted, still moving

towards her.

'Certainly not!' Sheena snapped out. 'Only that you're wasting your time. I told you that before, didn't I? All right, go ahead. I don't suppose I can stop you, but just remember that Milly's liable to walk in at any moment and is sure to tell Gran what she sees.'

'Milly's gone to bed,' Brad said smoothly. 'It wouldn't have mattered if she had been around. Remember Gran's pipe-dream? She hasn't dropped it yet, in spite of her assertion that folk ought to make up their own minds. I rather think she would welcome the news,' he added, as he reached her and jerked her into his arms.

Sheena's thoughts at that time were not on the fact that Brad was crushing her to him, but that he intended using Gran's hopes to make another conquest. She didn't believe for one moment that he had suddenly found her attractive. As Gran had said, he just wasn't used to competition. As his hard lips descended on hers, Sheena decided to give as good as she got. She wouldn't enjoy the experience, but on the other hand she was feminine enough to want to show him that two could play at that game. She could hold her own with him or with any man who thought that she was a pushover.

As her lips relaxed under his, and her stiff body became pliant, she felt the shock-waves go through him, and as their eyes met she saw his widen for a split second before his lips found hers again. This time the kiss was not hard and brutal but deep and searching, and he lightly traced the line of her mouth. 'Well, well,' he said softly, 'as I thought, you're not quite so innocent as you appear. Drop Dean Walling, and be nice to me. We could have a lot of fun, and you won't lose out on anything, I promise you.'

Sheena felt the shock-waves this time. She had been under a spell, and had totally misjudged her feelings on what she should have felt when Brad kissed her. Oh, no, she wouldn't enjoy the experience! Not only had she enjoyed it, but she hadn't wanted it to end, and here he was promising her a good time with, no doubt, monetary recompense for favours given! That was what he had meant about biting the hand that fed her! Somehow she kept her voice light as she answered him. 'Oh, come on,' she said, 'give up the chance of becoming a millionaire's wife? You don't think I'm that stupid, do you?'

Brad's eyes were hooded as he said softly, 'He won't marry you. Like Gran, you're having a pipe-dream.'

'Well, we'll see, won't we?' Sheena replied, her voice no longer light but cold. She hated this man for the yearning he had awoken in her. She had read about such feelings, but had never experienced them herself until now. In those few vital seconds she had become a woman, with a woman's feelings and needs, brought about by a man who had no respect for her. She felt cheated and degraded. 'In any case, I don't see what I've got to lose. On the other hand,' she said maliciously, 'I don't fancy your proposal.'

Brad broke in here with a growled, 'That'll be the day.'

'All right!' Sheena bit back. 'That was an unfortunate phrase. I got the message all right, don't worry, but I'd rather trust Dean than you, any day. So far I haven't let him touch me, but it will be interesting to see if he's as good as you are when it comes to physical persuasion. I've a feeling that I'm not going to be disappointed!'

Brad muttered an oath and lunged at her, holding her with suffocating tightness close to his hard body, then suddenly flung her away from him. 'Go ahead,' he snarled. 'See if I care. I shall just be an interested bystander from now on.' Then he stamped out of the room.

Sheena sat down slowly on the nearest lounge chair. She felt shaky and very unsure of herself, and, worse than that, wanted to cry her heart out. It wasn't a bit like her. Normally she would have had no patience with herself for showing such weakness. At that moment however, she couldn't conjure up any defence, not even a hint of indignation at the way Brad had treated her. She thought about Mary again, not quite half-way through her holiday, so there was no hope there of an early release from her predicament. A lot could happen in a week, she thought ruefully.

It was the thought of Mary that finally broke her misery and made her snap out of her lethargy. Slowly her shoulders straightened and the old glint of battle returned to her green eyes. So he wanted a fight, did he? In fact he was spoiling for one. Well, he would have one! She wasn't half a Muldoon for nothing! He had almost succeeded in battling down her defences, but then she was inexperienced in the ways of courtship. What she had taken for love turned out to be a schoolgirl crush, much as any student nurse would have had for her tutor.

If Brad Muldoon thought she was experienced, then so much the better. She wouldn't stand a chance with him if he knew the truth, so just for once she had the advantage. She meant to keep it!

Apart from the arrival of a highly coloured postcard from Mary the following morning the day passed without any other incident. Gran seemed lost in a reverie of her own making, and what little Sheena saw of Brad convinced her that he regarded her as about as palatable as yesterday's leftovers. Between Gran's reveries and Brad's disregard for her presence, Sheena felt like a displaced person who had been suddenly dropped among them. Neither seemed to know what she was doing there.

Friday couldn't arrive too soon for Sheena. She badly needed to feel wanted by someone, even if it was Dean Walling. He might for all she knew be playing the same game with her as Brad was with Glenda. Brad thought so, and on the face of things it did seem likely, but recalling the evenings she had spent with him Sheena found it hard to believe.

He hadn't had to propose to her, had he? He was no youth in the first flush of emotion. He knew what he was doing. Her smooth forehead creased as she put the finishing touches to her hair before going to join Brad, who was bound to be pacing up and down the hall waiting to take her to the dinner. There was one way to call his bluff, she told herself, and that was to accept his offer.

As soon as the thought was there, so was revulsion

for even considering such an action. Her wide eyes met their reflection in the dressing-table mirror. That was the effect Brad Muldoon had on her, she told herself. She might want to get back at him, but there was a limit to what she would do to get her revenge. Accepting his proposal was not only mean, it was despicable!

Brad's swift glance at her apparel when she finally got down to the hall said what it had said before: Hadn't she done well from Gran's generosity? The creamy silk suit with chocolate accessories fitted her slim figure like a glove, and would have gladdened its maker's heart to see it displayed to such advantage. None of this occurred to Sheena, who swept by the impatient Brad, calling out a 'See you' to Gran who would be taking up her usual stance at the lounge windows to see them off.

During dinner, Sheena found herself placed next to Glenda, who occupied the head of the table with Brad on her other side, directly facing Sheena who was grateful for the fact that Dean sat next to her.

The meal was lavish, in Sheena's opinion a bit too much so, and only a true gourmet would have appreciated it. She recalled reading somewhere that Glenda Walling was famed for her dinner parties, and this was no exception. The murmurs of appreciation as each dish was served were duly noted by Glenda, who glowed with pride at the compliments passed, and a bemused Sheena felt that it should have been the chef who received the compliments, not Glenda.

In between talking to Dean, and receiving

Glenda's effusive attention, not to mention Brad's studied attentiveness whenever she got into serious conversation with Dean, Sheena was only too pleased to rise from the table at the close of the meal and to take coffee in the lounge. A little dancing later provided for the guests' entertainment. There were fourteen people present, Leroy, happily for Sheena, not among them. She had enough to cope with without having to evade his attentions.

Brad and Glenda opened the dancing-session, and Dean and Sheena followed them on to the floor. Dean clasped Sheena's slim waist with a little more pressure than was necessary, and his attempt to dance cheek to cheek with her was rudely shattered by a collision with another couple. By chance this happened to be Brad and Glenda, and it so annoyed Dean that he said abruptly, 'Let's get out of this crush,' and guided Sheena off the floor and out of the french windows to the terraced gardens.

After they had walked some way away from the house, Dean stopped abruptly and gently pulled Sheena into his arms.

She was quite prepared for the kiss, in fact, she was really looking forward to it. No trouble there in making herself relax this time, she told herself confidently, as she accepted it.

To her intense annoyance however, she felt herself completely unable to respond in the way she should have done.

There was nothing wrong with Dean's kiss. His lips were firm and gentle. No hard bruising nor indeed any attempt to force her to respond. To Sheena's dismay it was about as exciting as a pat on the shoulder.

If Dean was disappointed, he did not show it, in fact commended her on her show of restraint. 'It's early days yet,' he said, 'and believe me, I think more of you because you didn't pretend to respond, as others would have done.'

At this point Brad appeared on the scene, standing before them with arms akimbo. 'Time we hit the road,' he said to Sheena 'I've a job to go to, remember?'

'Then you'd better be on your way,' Dean said firmly. 'I'll take Sheena home.'

Brad shook his head slowly. 'No go, I'm afraid. Gran wouldn't like that. I brought her, and I take her home.'

Sheena could sense the hostility building up between the two men, and felt a desire to see Dean land Brad one on the chin. His stance suggested he would dearly like to do so, but the commotion a fight would cause brought a measure of sense to her which won the day. 'I'm ready,' she said, and glanced at Dean, favouring him with a brilliant smile. 'See you on Sunday,' she said. 'This time we shall expect you to pick us up. I'm sure Brad would have made other arrangements,' she added sweetly.

'I shouldn't count on it,' Brad growled, as he shepherded her towards the house and cloakroom to collect her wrap.

There was a hostile silence between them on the way back, and in spite of Sheena's resolve not to get drawn into a slanging match, she suddenly recalled that the next day was Saturday, and couldn't help bursting out, 'Since when have you worked on a

Saturday?'

Brad's off-hand, 'Often. We don't work a five-day week in our job,' proved to her that she was getting precisely nowhere and she subsided into silence again.

'Did you enjoy it?' Brad suddenly asked.

Sheena looked at him briefly then turned her attention back to the dark passing scenery. 'I thought it was a very nice dinner,' she replied coldly.

'I wasn't referring to the dinner,' Brad said smoothly, 'I meant the kiss he gave you before I arrived on the scene.'

Sheena draw a deep breath. So much for her resolution not to get drawn into an argument with him! 'Of course I did,' she lied valiantly. 'I knew I would, and really, you shouldn't ask these questions, you know. It's not considered polite.'

'Didn't last long, did it?' Brad taunted softly, completely ignoring her rebuke.

'How do you know?' Sheena spat back angrily. 'You'd only just come on the scene. That wasn't the first kiss.'

'Liar!' Brad replied in a silky voice. 'I watched you both the whole time while you were out there. I told you I didn't trust the guy. After what I saw, I'm inclined to think it's his money the women go for!'

Sheena closed her eyes, and silently wished that she had a gun permit! Of all the hateful . . .! 'I wish Dean had landed you one,' she said between her teeth.

'If he ever does, then I hope he's fitter than he looks,' was the calm comment this statement produced. 'I can give him ten years, apart from a couple of beaut black eyes.'

Sheena chose to ignore this boastful promise, simply because it was probably true, and she couldn't bear it. 'And what was Glenda doing while you were doing your boy-scout act skulking in the bushes?' she demanded sarcastically.

From the faint light of the dashboard, she saw Brad grin and caught the white of his teeth. 'Sulking,' he said. 'They were playing her favourite dance tune when I made my departure.'

'Just how low can you get?' Sheena said angrily.

'Oh, I can get a damn sight lower if given enough provocation,' Brad said harshly. 'If you don't give Walling the push you'll find out. Oh, I can see your game all right. Keep them guessing, that's it, isn't it? You didn't exactly swoon in his arms, did you? Not the way you did with me. You're after a bigger game, and you're making all the right moves. I wouldn't care a damn, only I don't intend to see the family go through the divorce courts with all the accompanying mud-slinging, just to get you a rosy future. I'd even marry you myself to avoid that,' he threatened.

'Chance would be a fine thing!' Sheena all but shouted at him. 'And I'm a Fairburn, not a Muldoon.'

'You're a Muldoon!' Brad shouted back at her before bringing the car to a fast halt outside Grasslands. Both of them had been too involved in their quarrel to notice that they had almost overshot the driveway.

CHAPTER SEVEN

SHEENA got ready for bed in a white-hot fury. She would marry Dean, she fumed, as she threw off her clothes before a shower. If he asked her on Sunday, she would say yes, and to the devil with Brad Muldoon!

What more could she want of a man? she asked herself, as she got into bed. He was kind and attentive. He would give her time to adjust. She thumped the pillows behind her, wishing they were Brad Muldoon's head. Thinking of the scandal a divorce would bring the family, indeed, she fumed. More likely thinking along the lines that someone had scored where he hadn't! And wouldn't she enjoy announcing the news!

She settled down to sleep, but sleep wouldn't come. She tried to picture herself married to Dean, but somehow the scene wouldn't come to life. She turned restlessly, and sighed. It was no good. She was indulging in fancies. Much as she hated to agree with anything Brad had said, he had been absolutely right on this, though not for the reason he gave.

She couldn't marry Dean, because she didn't love him. Some women would be content with a secure future, but not her. It was as simple as that, and she couldn't go on cheating him. Sooner or later, he would realise that no matter how much time they had, it wouldn't happen. Not for her.

She sighed deeply. She would have to tell him, but in her own way, and not to accommodate Brad Muldoon's wishes. Then, she told herself, she would have to get Gran to agree to let her go home. She could say that she was homesick. Any excuse would do that helped her to put as much distance between herself and that obnoxious man as was humanly possible.

At breakfast the next morning, Sheena waited impatiently for Brad's departure, meaning to tackle Gran about going home. When she saw with growing annoyance that he was taking his time over his breakfast, she couldn't help asking acidly, 'Aren't you going to be late for work?'

Gran and Brad looked at her, then Brad helped himself to another cup of coffee before replying calmly, 'I've nothing on this morning. Do you fancy a trip out somewhere?'

For this kind offer, Gran gave Brad an approving nod, but Sheena could have screamed. 'No, thank you!' she replied tightly. 'It must be nice to have the kind of job you've got, deciding whether to go in or not.'

Gran looked at her. 'Brad never works weekends. I can't recall when he ever did,' she said with a frown.

'According to what he said last night,' Sheena replied accusingly, 'he was going in this morning. It was his excuse for bringing me home early.'

'Early?' Brad queried with uplifted brows. 'I wouldn't call one-thirty early.'

Gran's eyes went from Sheena to Brad. 'Have you two been quarrelling again?' she said sternly.

Sheena looked away from the amusement in Brad's eyes as he replied lazily,' We just don't see eye to eye on a few things, Gran. Nothing serious, you know. I'm working on it.'

Sheena's eyes flashed. 'We don't see eye to eye on anything. Gran, and we never will!' she declared grimly, as she got up from the table and left them to it. No matter what, she couldn't win where Brad Muldoon was concerned. Already he had twisted events to suit his purpose. The next thing she knew, Gran would be giving her a lecture and asking her to try to get on with Brad!

Back in her room she closed her door with a snap of finality. She wouldn't go down again until Brad had gone, if it meant staying where she was all morning. There was no hope of a talk with Gran with him hanging around. She sighed. There were things she could tell her, and some she couldn't, and Brad's dubious offer was one of the things she couldn't tell her.

For want of something to do, she sat down to write to Mary, although she knew she wouldn't get the letter until she returned from her holiday. The most important thing was to warn Mary that she hoped to be coming home very soon, and could she have her old room back until she had got herself fixed up in the nurses' hostel again. She saw no problem here, there were always vacancies in the hostel, and if by any chance they were full she could always share with someone until a room became vacant.

She managed to inject some enthusiasm into the letter in spite of her frustrations, ending with a cryptic, 'I'm afraid I'm not cut out for socialising;

I'd rather be back at work.'

At this point she heard Brad's car start up, and she sealed her letter and went down to the lounge to find Gran ensconced in her chair and settling down to her crochet again.

'You know, Sheena, you ought to have accepted Brad's offer this morning,' she said, as Sheena appeared. 'He really is trying to get to know you.'

Sheena had expected this rebuke and took it in her stride. 'I don't see the point of going anywhere with him when we quarrel all the time,' she said reasonably.

Gran tut-tutted. 'But at least he's trying,' she said sternly, 'and you're not helping by putting his back up, are you?'

Sheena drew in a deep breath. 'Look, Gran, we may as well face it. Brad and I are like fire and water. We don't mix, and never will,' she stated flatly.

Gran looked up from her work. 'He's sitting up and taking notice, isn't he?' she said. 'If I didn't know better, I'd say you were playing a deep game with him, and if you really wanted to, you'd land him without a struggle.'

This was the last straw for Sheena. 'Gran!' she said angrily. 'You're not still clinging to that old hope of yours, are you? Nothing, but nothing, would make me say yes to that man to anything, let alone a proposal.'

'Did you say that you didn't want a spin out?' Brad's smooth voice intervened at this point, and caused some confusion, for neither of them had heard him come back. All Sheena could think of at that time was that she was once again denied a

long talk with Gran about going home. 'Yes!' she
shouted back at him, not caring whether it was polite
or not.

It was only afterwards that she realised what had
happened. She knew for certain that Brad had heard
what she had said to Gran, and could have wept with
frustration at the way he had once again shot her
down. She hadn't missed Gran's amusement either,
for she had caught on quicker than Sheena had as to
what Brad was up to.

It seemed an age before Brad finally left them
together, and wasting no time, Sheena tackled her
about letting her go home. 'I feel so useless here,'
she said, 'and I'm homesick, Gran.'

'You can't go yet,' Gran said calmly. 'Mary's still
away, isn't she? Where will you stay? Why not wait
until she's back, and we'll have another talk about
it,' she advised her.

That was as far as Sheena got, and what she
would have to agree to, whether she liked it or not,
She had got somewhere, though she told herself, for
Gran couldn't keep putting her off, not after Mary
was back home.

Dean called for them just after seven on the
Sunday, and Sheena did not miss the way he
glanced around as if expecting Brad to put in an
appearance. He seemed relieved at his absence.
Sheena could have told him that he had taken
himself off to a civic meeting, after probably
receiving a warning from Gran to keep his distance.
Not that that would have had much effect, but for
the fact that Gran was included in the invitation.
Her presence would surely curtail any amorous

moves by Dean, for that was the way Brad Muldoon
would see it, Sheena thought shrewdly.

Gran's presence certainly did curtail Dean's hope
of furthering his cause with Sheena, but he bore up
very well, she thought, and never gave the
impression that he would rather be enjoying a solo
date with Sheena than entertaining her grandmother.

It was a quiet dinner with just the three of them,
and Sheena felt a stab of conscience at the thought
that they were there under false pretences. She
wished that they were on their own so that she could
give Dean his answer. He wasn't going to like it, but
then she had never given him cause to believe that
his quest was going to be successful.

From what she knew of Dean, Sheena could not
see him calmly accepting the situation. He was not
that kind of a man. He liked his own way, as Brad
Muldoon did. In fact, they were two of a kind, she
thought, as she watched Dean help Gran into his car
before taking them home at a very respectable hour.

He did, however, manage to have a few private
words with Sheena after Gran had gone in to
Grasslands. 'I'm off up north tomorrow to see some
bloodstock that have come on the market,' he said.
'I should only be away a day. I'll give you a ring on
Tuesday, anyway, and fix a date.' He gave her a
quick hug and a sedate kiss on her forehead, then
just before he got into his car, he turned back to her
and said, 'Look, watch out for that Brad Muldoon.
He's got his eye on you, and it's nothing to do with
family connections either.' With a wave he was
off.

As if I didn't know, Sheena thought, as she went into the house. She was surprised to find Brad settled in one of the lounge chairs ostensibly reading a paper, and asking Gran how she had enjoyed herself.

'That man knows how to entertain his guests,' she replied graciously. 'We both enjoyed the dinner, didn't we, Sheena?'

Sheena had no difficulty in supporting this statement, but refrained from elaboration on the subject, not wanting to start another fight.

'And I suppose he's seeing you tomorrow?' Brad asked Sheena smoothly.

While Sheena caught her breath, Gran saved her the trouble of replying. 'That's nothing to do with you, Brad. That's Sheena's business.'

Brad gave Gran a pitying look. 'It's everything to do with me,' he said harshly. 'She's family, remember. I've warned her, and I'm warning you. Dean Walling is bad news as far as I'm concerned, and as long as I'm head of this family, that's the way it's going to stay. Now is he seeing you, or not?' he shot out at Sheena.

'No, he is not!' Sheena replied angrily. 'At least, not tomorrow. He's off up north to see some bloodstock. Not that it's any business of yours, as Gran said, but I shall certainly be seeing him after that whether you like it or not!'

'So he's off to that sale, too, is he?' Brad mused, quite ignoring Sheena's show of defiance. 'Got his eye on Midnight Prairie, I'll be bound, and I was rather hoping to make a bid there myself. Still, we'll see,' he ended, much to Gran and Sheena's bemusement, and Sheena took the opportunity of going while the going was good, and went to her room for an early night.

Some time during the early hours of the morning Sheena thought she heard a car start up, but it was only a vague impression clouded by sleep.

Gran's 'Brad left in the early hours to go to that auction' confirmed her vague recollections. 'I hope he didn't disturb you,' Gran went on. 'I'm a light sleeper myself. In any case, I was awake.'

Sheena assured her that she had not been disturbed. 'I did hear something,' she said, 'but I was too tired to take much notice of it.'

'I do hope those two don't come to blows over that colt Brad's got his eye on,' Gran said, as she sipped her orange juice. She frowned at Milly, who had just knocked a coffee-cup askew before filling it, and made little twittering noises as she righted it. 'Not that I'm worried about Brad being able to look after himself,' she went on smoothly, and Milly's hand that had been a little shaky pouring the coffee steadied with remarkable agility.

When she had left the room, Gran remarked wryly, 'I'm afraid Milly's affection for Brad makes one have to watch one's words, and he really doesn't deserve it, you know. He's the child she never had, I suppose, but no matter what, she's on his side through thick and thin.'

Sheena's thoughts were not on Milly's adoration of Bred, but on what Gran had said earlier. 'You don't really think they'll fight, do you?' she asked anxiously.

Gran buttered a thin slice of toast. 'There's no

doubt that Brad's itching for a chance of a scrap with him,' she said, 'and it's nothing to do with bloodstock.'

Sheena stared down at her half-eaten breakfast. Her appetite had suddenly deserted her. 'It's not fair!' she said in a low voice.

Gran looked at her. 'All's fair in love and war, you ought to know that,' she said.

'But it's not love!' Sheena cried out angrily. 'It's not love, it's pride. Dean doesn't love me. He only sees someone he feels would make him a good wife. As for Brad Muldoon——' she drew in a deep breath '—that's where pride comes in, Gran. He knows that I don't like him and he simply can't take it. It's as simple as that!'

'Is it?' Gran queried, her faded blue eyes studying Sheena. 'You've two men fighting over you, girl. I only hope you make the right decision.'

Sheena did not intend to join in Gran's pipe-dream however flattering it was. 'Stuff and nonsense!' she said, making Gran smile in appreciation at hearing her favourite saying quoted back at her. 'They're two stupid men who like having their own way and I just happen to have got caught in the cross-fire! Oh, do stop laughing, Gran! I'm being perfectly honest.'

'You're a true Muldoon,' said Gran fondly, patting her hand.

'Now don't you start!' Sheena said. 'Why, I'd rather put up with Leroy,' she added darkly.

'Has he proposed too?' Gran asked in surprise.

'Of course not!' Sheena replied caustically. 'He's too afraid of his mother. At least, that's what Brad said, and I'm inclined to believe him.'

A depressed Sheena and a highly amused Gran
left the breakfast table for the lounge, Sheena to read
some magazines and Gran to her crochet.

As if summoned by a genie, Leroy rang her up
later that morning wondering if she was free to have
dinner with him that evening. In a fit of boredom
Sheena agreed, regretting it shortly afterwards, but
she managed to console herself with the thought that
even Leroy's absorption with Leroy was better than
having to put up with Gran's complacent outlook
through those rose-coloured glasses that she simply
refused to take off.

Now that Leroy's position in Sheena's affection
was clear to Gran she had no objection to Sheena's
having dinner with him, and this depressed Sheena
too.

The evening passed by as Sheena had predicted,
with Leroy expounding on the exploits of Leroy. He
did manage to put in a sly hint on the unsuitability of
Dean Walling as a friend, making Sheena wonder if
Brad had put him up to it, and suggested that Leroy
should take her out. She wouldn't put it past him,
she thought, as she countered his warning with a
sweet smile, assuring him that she took folk as she
found them. Sensing her reluctance to continue the
subject, he returned to his favourite theme.

Sheena went down to breakfast the following
morning with the full expectation of finding that
Brad had been in a fight. If he had it certainly did
not show on his rugged, handsome features. Sheena
did not know whether to be pleased or disappointed
about this, but she did wonder about Dean.

'Well, did you get the colt?' Gran asked the question Sheena wanted to ask but couldn't.

Brad smiled. Really, he was in a very good mood, Sheena thought with apprehension. She thought she knew the answer before he gave it.

'As a matter of fact, I didn't,' Brad replied, helping himself to another slice of toast. 'Walling was fighting it out with an oilman, and the stakes were getting too high for my liking. I believe Walling won—on that occasion.' He favoured Gran with another smile, but his eyes were on Sheena.

Now what did he mean by that? Sheena wondered, but the relief that had gone through her at the knowledge that they had not come to blows far overrode any other consideration, and she did not dwell on it. She would be hearing from Dean herself some time today, she reminded herself, so it was not important.

Gradually Tuesday slipped by, and Sheena was still waiting for a call from Dean. The thought did occur to her that he might have been held up making arrangements to have the colt delivered to his home. Even so, surely he would have let her know?

A week later, there was still no message from Dean. Sheena came to the conclusion that away from familiar surroundings he had suddenly realised his mistake in proposing to a woman he barely knew. Perhaps he had been to a party—there were always parties held on those occasions—and had met someone he liked better. In fact it could be anything, but if the truth were told Sheena was relieved. She was saved the trouble of refusing him, and would not have to worry about any comeback through his determination to get his own way.

Throughtout this period Sheena found herself the recipient of Brad's studious attentions. She found this even more of a nuisance than his earlier treatment of her. She didn't trust him, and was sure that he was putting on a show for Gran's benefit. It was very astute of him, but didn't fool her for a moment.

No mention was made of Dean Walling, and Sheena was made to feel like the deserted woman. In deference to her feelings the subject was taboo!

Womanlike, she resented this, and would have liked a chance to prove to both of them that she had had no intention of marrying Dean, but even this small consolation was denied her.

She could, however, still stand her ground with Brad Muldoon, and she politely refused every invitation he threw her way to attend this or that function. If they thought it was because of Dean, then all to the good, but she certainly wasn't letting herself in for another of his persuasive attacks on her emotions. She couldn't trust him to behave once they were alone, and to be perfectly frank, she couldn't trust herself not to respond in a manner that was quite out of keeping with her normal sense of propriety. She would never forgive herself if she did succumb, for this was all he was waiting for. Once he had captured her heart he would lose interest in her.

Mary was now back home, and Sheena's hopes of going home received another setback when Gran complained of slight chest pains and took to her bed.

The doctor said it was nothing to worry about,

and all she needed to do was to take things easy. In fact, he remarked to Sheena, Mrs Muldoon was in remarkably good health for her age, and he saw no cause for alarm. In a few days she should be back on her feet again.

The doctor's assurances brought some relief to Sheena. It also brought some speculation as to whether Gran had really been unwell, or was just shamming to keep Sheena at Grasslands. There was no doubt that she was quite capable of using such tactics, particularly if she had convinced herself that Brad was in love with Sheena.

If she was shamming, then this was a ploy that would be used again whenever the occasion demanded, such as Sheena's threatened departure. There was nothing that Sheena could do about it, because she couldn't be absolutely certain that Gran was playing up. It was certainly true that she had had a lot of amusement that could be classed as excitement since Sheena's arrival, but Sheena had a sneaking feeling that it would take more than this to upset Gran's constitution.

There was, of course, one way she could settle this problem once and for all, and that was to give in to Brad Muldoon, accept his invitation, and see the whole thing through. That would take courage, and Sheena didn't feel she was strong enough to withstand the onslaught. She had no wish to return home pining for a man who would already have forgotten her existence.

At this thought she pulled herself up. What on earth was she drivelling on about? How could she pine for a man like Brad Muldoon? She hated him, didn't she? If she loved him, she wasn't going to admit it in a thousand years!

But whatever the answer, she was not prepared to put it to the test. All she had to do was to stick it out. Sooner or later, Brad would lose patience and turn his attentions elsewhere. Gran would then accuse her of losing her chance with him. Well, she could put up with that, it was better that way than that Gran should find out that Brad's intentions were not the same as hers.

During the next few weeks, Sheena occasionally accepted an invitation from Leroy, but she managed to avoid having a whole evening with him, on the grounds of not wanting to leave her grandmother alone. This wasn't quite true, for Milly was there, and would have been very upset had she heard Sheena's excuse but it served her purpose. Leroy, who had been well trained on family commitments by his mother, accepted the situation without a murmur.

As she did not wish to embarrass Dean or his daughter, Sheena only accepted invitations to places where she would not be likely to run into either of them.

There was bound to be a time, however, when this careful scheme went awry. It happened in a restaurant where Leroy had taken her to lunch. Just as she was about to take her seat she saw him wave to someone in a far corner of the room. Glancing that way, she saw that it was Glenda, and she sat down quickly, grateful for the thick arrangement of flowers that separated the tables and completely screened her from view.

She was certain that Glenda had seen her. If she wanted to have a few words with her then the occasion was there, but considering everything Sheena thought it more likely that she would keep her distance. It couldn't have been the first time that she had run into one of her father's ex-girlfriends, so she must have had plenty of practice!

When they were about to leave the restaurant Glenda approached them, and she cut short Leroy's cheerful greeting by directly addressing Sheena, 'Could I have a few words with you?' she asked in a tone that soundly slightly belligerent. She indicated that they should go to the powder room, and Sheena, following her, realised that her apparent belligerence was in fact embarrassment at her father's inconsiderate treatment of her. Sheena meant to spare her a few uncomfortable moments by assuring her that she had no cause to worry on her behalf, and that she had more or less expected something like this to happen, and she wished she and her father well.

As it happened, Sheena did not have an opportunity to express any of these sentiments. Glenda's first words when they were alone put quite a different complexion on the matter. 'I suppose you thought that was clever, did you?' she all but hissed at Sheena. 'So my father did play around a bit, but there was no need to make him look a fool!'

Sheena's eyes widened. 'I don't——' she began.

'Oh, no, of course not! You've no idea what I'm talking about, have you?' Glenda said acidly. 'Thanks to Brad Muldoon, who saw fit to put father into the picture, you could have gone on with your little game. Not that it fooled me for a moment. I knew there was something between you two the moment I set eyes on you. Distant cousin you may be, but you're also Brad's woman.'

'Is that what he told you?' Sheena asked, while Glenda was drawing breath.

'It's what he told my father,' Glenda said. 'No matter what you say, I believe it, and so does he. It explained so many things that didn't add up. Well, now you know that we're wise to you,' she ended, and turned on her heel. 'I just wanted you to know that you've been rumbled, and when Brad gets tired of you, don't bother to contact my father. Once bitten, twice shy, as they say.' She made for the door.

Her hand was turning the handle when Sheena managed to collect her reeling senses enough to ask breathlessly, 'Did he say why it was so necessary to keep this affair we're supposed to be having so quiet?'

Glenda gave her a pitying look. 'Afraid it will get to your grandmother's ears?' she suggested coldly. 'I'd worked that one out for myself. You're not exactly in the right social class for a Muldoon to marry, are you? So I shouldn't put any hope in that direction if I were you. Mrs Muldoon would expect a more advantageous match for him, and Brad knows it. Does that answer your question?' With that she left.

Sheena just stood where she was. So that was why Brad Muldoon had looked so pleased with himself when he had returned from that auction! He hadn't wanted that colt at all, just the chance to have a few private words with Dean.

She felt the heat rise in her cheeks at the thought of what Brad might have told Dean. He had said he could sink much lower if the occasion warranted it, hadn't he? Well, he'd surely got to the bottom this time!

On the way home, Sheena did not hear a word Leroy was saying. He could have asked her to elope with him for all she knew! Glenda's words kept going round and round in her head.

Although shocked, she had to admit that Brad had not only outwitted her, but outclassed her, and thoroughly destroyed any chance she might have had of accepting Dean's proposal. The fact that she had had no intention of marrying Dean was beside the point; it was the way that he had manoeuvred events to suit his purpose that took Sheena's breath away.

Not only had he removed a rival, he had paved the way for his future hopes where she was concerned. Glenda had been right in one thing, and that was that Brad had no intention of marrying her. That however was the only fact that she had got right, Sheena thought sardonically.

She was certainly way off course where Gran's hopes were concerned, and her eyes narrowed as a possible solution hit her. What better way to explain to Dean the need to keep the affair she was supposed to be having with him under wraps than to hint at his grandmother's displeasure should it come to light! No wonder Dean had believed him. That way it made perfect sense.

Sheena's lower teeth caught her upper lip. Well,

he wasn't going to get away with it. She wasn't going to play his little game. If only there had been someone else—she glanced at Leroy happily expounding on some event that had caught his imagination. 'Why haven't you married, Leroy?' she asked. The car swerved violently for a second until he had got it under control again and he cast a very wary eye at Sheena who had to laugh. 'Don't worry. I didn't mean it personally,' she went on. 'It's just that I'm a bit fed up. So much emphasis seem to be put on marriage these days, as if it's all we should be aiming at. Well, it is, of course, but I think it's more important to find the right one first, don't you?'

Leroy took a deep breath. 'Couldn't agree more,' he replied lightly. 'Mother talks of nothing else, you know,' he added gloomily. 'Seems to think that I can take my pick of a bunch of socialites. Well, got to have the right background, you know.'

'Does she know you're seeing me?' Sheena asked with a grin.

Leroy's brows rose. 'Of course she does!' he replied as if anything else was unthinkable.

'And she doesn't object?' Sheena persisted.

'No, why should she?' he said. 'She knows you're half a Muldoon, and that's good enough for her. She has quite a lot of respect for your grandmother, you know,' he added.

Sheena's eyes narrowed. So much for Brad's sarcastic remarks on Mrs Leroy's attitude towards her son getting interested in her!

'That's the trouble, you see,' Leroy went on soulfully. 'My wishes don't come into it.'

Sheena stared at him. 'Leroy, is there someone you do care for?' she asked.

He nodded gloomily. 'A beaut of a brunette mother wouldn't allow to cross over the threshold. She works in a tobacconist's shop.' He gave Sheena a swift glance, not at all Leroy-like, and Sheena felt that she was only now seeing the real man. 'You won't mention this, will you?' he asked anxiously. 'Mother would whisk me off to the Azores or some other outlandish place if she knew about Elena.'

Sheena was curious, and forgot her own troubles. 'How long have you known her?' she asked.

'Three years,' Leroy replied glumly

Sheena stared at him. 'Three whole years?' she exclaimed in amazement, and as the car neared Grasslands, she said impulsively, 'Look, Leroy, we'll talk about this. Let's go out to one of the parks.'

Leroy sensed that Sheena wanted to help him and wasn't just interested for curiosity's sake. He drove on past Grasslands and towards the parks.

When they found a secluded area and pulled up, Sheena said, 'Now, Leroy, you must do something about this. You can't go on pleasing your mother.'

'No choice,' Leroy replied miserably.

'Are you sure of this Elena?' she asked.

Leroy looked at her. 'It's one of those things,' he said. 'You can't explain it. I knew from the start she was the girl for me. She hasn't threatened me or tried to force things. We see each other when we can, but I have to be careful. What I usually do is leave parties early and go and see her. I would have got her to come and see me when Mother was away, you know when you came that time, but that sneak of a butler would have told Mother. She heard about your visits.'

'Why don't you stand up to your mother?' Sheena asked.

Leroy blinked. 'You mean tell her about Elena?' he asked with a horrified expression on his face at the very thought. 'You can't mean that. If you knew my mother——'

'She's human, isn't she?' Sheena said, although going by the look Leroy gave her he was not too sure of this. 'All right, then. What do you intend to do? Marry someone of your mother's choosing? She will find someone for you, you know,' Sheena added firmly. 'Have you money of your own?' This explanation suddenly occurred to her.

Leroy looked indignant. 'Of course I have,' he said. 'But it's not that at all. It's just that Mother has a weak heart and it plays her up.'

'When you don't do what she wants you to do?' Sheena suggested with a twinkle in her eye. Shades of Gran, she thought.

Leroy nodded dolefully.

'In that case you'll go on for years as you are doing,' Sheena said remorselessly, 'and you'll eventually marry someone your mother approves of, and Elena will marry someone else, and you'll neither of you live happily ever after.'

'But I don't see what else we can do,' he said miserably.' On the one hand there's Mother who would make life miserable for Elena if she found out about her, and on the other hand there's Elena's aunt, she owns the store Elena works in, and she doesn't like me very much. She's always inviting Elena to tea over the weekends, and trying to get her interested in other men by inviting them over at the same time. Not that I blame her, she's looking out for Elena's happiness.'

'Well, there's only one thing to be done,' Sheena said firmly. 'You must marry your Elena and there's an end to it.'

'Mother would never——' Leroy began.

'Your mother wouldn't know until it was all over. Get a special licence, Leroy. Once it's done there's nothing your mother can do about it. For once in your life face up to her. I don't advise you to live at home, either. Find a place of your own. So your mother will play up, or her heart will, but that's predictable. When she sees that that's not getting her anywhere she'll start to make the best of things, if she really cares for you. Either way, you can't lose, can you?'

Leroy stared at her with open mouth. 'Do you really think it would work?' he said tentatively.

'It will if you make it,' Sheena replied. 'All you have to do is plan ahead. Take an early summer vacation. No doubt Elena has holidays, too. Surely you can work something out between you'

Leroy's shoulders straightened, and a gleam came into his eyes. 'I only wish I'd met you three years ago,' he said. 'You can't think what it's been like attending all those functions and hating every minute of it. Oh, I know what they all think of me, but I didn't care as long as Elena was there. I had to be careful not to get involved with anyone else, just

show enough interest to put Mother off the scent.'
His face fell as a thought suddenly occurred to him.

'What's wrong?' Sheena aked.

'First snag,' Leroy said? 'The set's off on an
outback tour next week, and I shall be expected to go
with them. I'd forgotten I'd already made the
arrangements.'

'Well, cancel them,' Sheena said. 'If you want a
good excuse, make out you're still interested in me.
I'm only here on a visit, remember, and could go
home at any time.'

'Are you sure——?' Leroy began.

'Of course I don't mind. In fact, you'll be doing
me a favour, too, Leroy. There are reasons why I
need to be away from Grasslands as much as
possible during the next few weeks. All you have to
do is pick me up every day and drop me off
somewhere, then collect me later in the day. You
can then get on with arranging things your end.
Looking for a house for starters, not forgetting to
arrange the licence. As for me, I'll be looking for a
place I can rent for a week or so during the daytime
to catch up on my studies.'

It was now Sheena's turn to do a little explaining.
She told Leroy about her hopes of passing her
Finals, and how impossible it was to study at
Grasslands. 'Gran doesn't really understand that
it's what I want to do,' she ended, 'and I've already
lost a few weeks' swotting.'

The upshot of this confidence was entirely satisfying from both points of view. Leroy suggested that
Sheena used Elena's flat for her work, where she
could be certain of no distractions, assuring her of

Elena's co-operation when she heard Leroy's news. 'She'll be as grateful as I am for your help,' he said happily.

There remained one more thing Sheena had to guard against, and that was that Leroy did not divulge any of this to anyone. She laid stress on 'anyone', but was thinking particularly of Brad Muldoon. She knew that Leroy had a great respect for Brad and said, 'Remember that if it got to Grandmother's ear, she might just think it a good thing to put your mother into the picture.' She added this for good measure, and by the horrified look Leroy gave at this probability she felt sure that he would keep his side of the bargain.

CHAPTER EIGHT

SHEENA went back to Grasslands feeling much happier than she had felt for weeks. Thank goodness she had had the foresight to bring her books with her, in the belief that she would have plenty of time to study. Now at last things were going her way.

No one, but no one, was going to stop her doing what she wanted to do, for once Brad Muldoon had done her a favour by putting an end to her association with Dean Walling.

She would have enjoyed actually telling him so, but she was bound by the same ties as Leroy, and this was one luxury she would have to forgo. She could, of course, have a go at him over the way he had bounced Dean out of her life, but as the eventual outcome had landed in her favour, the less said the better.

It was Brad who was going to lose out in the long run when the news got around that she was seeing a lot of Leroy. It was bound to start a bit of speculation in that direction, and this alone was ample reward for Sheena.

Things, she thought cheerfully, were definitely looking up for her, and couldn't have worked out better. The fact that Leroy had not probed further into the fact that she needed to be away from Grasslands told its own story, and she was sure that he thought that it was Dean she was trying to avoid.

He would have been very surpised to learn that it was Brad!

Now that Sheena was out of what had been a very muddled situation, she was able to look back with a spurt of surprise at how much had happened to her since her arrival in Canberra.

A proposal from a man she barely knew, followed by a very suggestive one from Brad Muldoon that wasn't worth a second thought, and finally Leroy, who was anything but the bore he appeared to be in society.

It seemed, she thought ruefully, that she had the knack of attracting the would-be drop-outs from the eternal social roundabout.

Dean had made a dead set at her because of her no-nonsense outlook on life, not to mention the fact that she had no mercenary designs.

Leroy had sought her company for more or less the same reasons, sensing that here was someone that he could safely escort around without finding himself enmeshed by an up-and-coming socialite on the lookout for a socially acceptable husband. There were plenty of those around, she thought, and marvelled at the way that he had managed to sidestep any such attempts for as long as he had. But then, there had been Elena, and surely that was the real thing?

Finally, there was Brad Muldoon, but there was no mystery there. Just a case of an overinflated ego!

As Brad did not put in an appearance at dinner that evening, it did occur to Sheena that he might have heard of her confrontation with Glenda and decided that discretion was the better part of valour.

He might be waiting until she cooled down before he joined the family again.

However satisfying this thought was, Sheena could not believe it. He was too sure of himself to skulk in a corner when trouble was brewing. He was more likely to enjoy the fight, she thought, but then a second explanation occurred to her that certainly would explain his absence.

He would have no qualms about tackling her, but Gran was a different proposition. Whether she was on his side or not, she would not take kindly to the suggestion that Sheena was his mistress, whichever way you put it. That was what Glenda had implied, and certainly what she believed, and worse than that, what Brad must have intimated to Dean.

He must, Sheena thought musingly after dinner, as they sat in the lounge, Gran with her crochet and her supposedly reading a book, have a great deal more faith in her integrity than he had previously given her credit for. Here was an occasion for her to gain the initiative and expose his double-dealing where she was concerned.

She frowned. It wasn't a bit like him to overlook such a possibility, and she felt there must be a catch to it. Whatever it was it certainly wouldn't turn out in her favour. Sheena had a lot of respect for Brad's deviousness, having learnt the hard way, so she was grateful that she did not have to accept whatever bait he was throwing her way. She was quite satisfied the way things were going.

'You're very quiet tonight, Sheena,' Gran said, casting her a look over the spectacles she wore for close work.

Sheena smiled at her. 'Well, things are quiet, aren't they, Gran?' she said. 'I'm not complaining, you know, in fact I prefer it this way.'

Gran nodded. 'Ay, you're a home girl, and that's no bad thing. You're not pining for that Dean, are you?' she asked suddenly.

Since this was the first time that Dean's name had been mentioned for a week or two, Sheena felt surprised that Gran should bring it up now. 'No, Gran,' she said. 'I told you how I felt about the whole thing. To tell you the truth I'm relieved that it's all over. He probably met someone when he was at that auction.'

'Didn't tell you though, did he?' Gran replied with a frown. 'Didn't do things like that in my day.'

'Well, I suppose it was a bit embarrassing for him,' Sheena said with a smile.

'It's not often I'm taken in,' Gran said, 'and I was sure that that man knew what he was about. You don't suppose that Brad——?'

Gran was fishing, Sheena thought, but decided to side-step that one. 'Oh. I shouldn't think so,' she replied quickly. 'I can't see Dean accepting any hints in that direction, can you? They weren't exactly on good terms, were they?'

Although not convinced of this, Gran had to leave it at that, but then started on a new tack. 'Seeing Leroy again, are you?' she asked idly.

Sheena nodded, glad of a change of topic, and of the chance to prepare the ground for the scheme she had hatched up with him. 'He's taking me out tomorrow,' she said.

'Can't see what you find to talk about with

him,' Gran grumbled. 'The man's an ass.'

'No, he's not!' Sheena replied in swift defence of
Leroy. 'He's like me, hates all the social occasions
he has to attend. It's only shyness that makes him
behave like a perfect bore. On his own he's a very
nice person.'

Gran looked alarmed. 'You're not getting serious
over him, are you?' she asked anxiously. 'I'm not so
sure that I wouldn't prefer the Walling crowd to that
awful mother of his, and believe me, you get Leroy,
you get his mother!'

Sheena chuckled. 'Oh, Gran, why do you always
think in terms of marriage? I haven't any such
thoughts in mind. No, I like Leroy because he's
Leroy, I suppose, and perfectly trustworthy. You've
nothing to worry about, I promise you.'

When Sheena got down to breakfast the next
morning, Brad had what she could only describe as
an expectant look on his face. Sheena surmised that
she hadn't been all that far out when she had
thought that he had something up his sleeve, and
that could only mean that there had been a purpose
behind his absence at dinner. Was she supposed to
spill the beans to Gran? Was that what he hoped
would happen? It didn't make any kind of sense to
Sheena, but whatever game he was playing she did
not intend to participate in it.

As no one seemed anxious to start the conversation, Gran decided to bring up the subject of
Leroy, much to the annoyance of Sheena. 'What
time is Leroy collecting you?' she asked, accom-
plishing two objectives at one hit. One to let Brad
know that she was still seeing Leroy, and two to

give him an opportunity of commenting on the fact.

Sheena just had time to say that she thought it would be around tennish before Brad said, 'Leroy's off an an outback trip next week, but as we've got our quarter sessions break coming up I'll see that you're entertained.'

Gran nodded her approval of this suggestion, but her smile of encouragement at Brad soon turned to a frown of displeasure at Sheena's calm, 'Thank you, Brad, but really there's no need to put yourself out. Leroy's decided to forgo that trip in order to see a little more of me. I shall soon be going home, you know, and I think it's very kind of him to want to entertain me, don't you?'

'Very kind,' Brad growled, in the tone of voice that boded ill for Leroy. 'Just remind him that your family has some claim on your time, will you? I shall expect your company at the close of sessions party on Wednesday. If he can spare you, that is,' he added ominously.

It went through Sheena's mind that you couldn't win them all, and she would have to attend that party with Brad, for as things stood she had no valid excuse to get out of it. It wouldn't be for the want of trying, she reminded herself.

Happily, Brad had departed for work long before Leroy called for her, and Sheena, armed with her nursing manuals which she had crammed into a small holdall, called a cheerful farewell to Gran before squeezing herself into his sports car, and they were off.

Sensing trouble ahead for Leroy, she put him into

the picture as far as Brad was concerned, warning
him that he might try and coerce him into fading out
of the picture, but to resist any such attempt. It
would not have done to have told him the real reason
for Brad's interest in her welfare, so she had to think
up some other reason. 'It's for Gran's sake, really,
Leroy,' she said. 'Brad feels that I ought to spend
more time with her, but on the other hand, Gran
wants me to enjoy myself and get about as much as
possible while I'm here. As long as I'm home
during the evenings, he hasn't a lot to complain
about.'

Leroy accepted this explanation without demur,
but he was a little concerned about upsetting Brad.
'Wouldn't want to get on the wrong side of Brad,' he
said. 'He's been good to me.'

Sheena assured him on this point, telling him that
as long as he told him that Sheena would be free
during the evening, he hadn't anything to worry
about. It would be she who would have to do the
worrying, she told herself privately, for with that
assurance Brad would be sure to press home his
advantage and swamp her with invitations for this
and that function, some of which she would have to
accept.

Her good idea wasn't turning out such a good
idea after all, she thought gloomily as the car sped to
Elena's flat. It was beginning to look like a case of
out of the frying-pan, into the fire! But surely the
fact that she was able to study was some compensation. She would have that behind her when Brad
had grown tired of the game.

At this point, his strong, handsome features rose

before her, with that all too knowing look of his that
sent shivers down her spine. Now he's haunting me,
she thought wretchedly, and she gave a sigh of
inward relief when they reached journey's end.
Elena lived in a block of flats like so many of the
buildings in Canberra, situated in landscaped
gardens. In early spring the buds of the flowering
bushes were about to make their début.

Elena had a flat on the ground floor, and to
Sheena's surprise was there when they arrived.

She was much as Leroy had described her, a
plump, pretty brunette, and rather shy, who
obviously adored Leroy. 'I'm doing some shopping
for my aunt,' she explained, as she led Sheena into
the apartment which had wide, airy rooms and a
very modern décor, 'so I can take my time in getting
in.' She broke off here and looked at Leroy. 'I've
managed to get next week off,' she said shyly. 'Aunt
Doris thinks that you're going on that trip to the
outback,' she added with a smile.

'Couldn't be better,' Leroy exclaimed happily,
and looked at Sheena. 'I rang Elena up last night
and put her in the picture.' He put an arm around
the plump brunette's shoulder. 'Gave her a bit of a
shock, I think, but as you see she's come through it,
as I knew she would.'

'Leroy said that you wanted some place to study,'
Elena said to Sheena, 'and you're welcome to use
my flat.' Her glance fell on a large abstract picture
that looked at if the artist had lost his inspiration
somewhere along the way. 'Goes with the flat, but
not to my taste, I'm afraid.'

Leroy squeezed her. 'You can pick your own

décor now, love,' he reminded her. 'I've applied for a special licence, so now we have to find a place, and we've a whole week to do it in,'

Sheena couldn't help feeling a spurt of envy at the look of blissful happiness on Elena's features.

'I don't know how to thank you,' Elena said to Sheena shyly. 'I don't think either of us would have dared——' she broke off and looked at Leroy. 'Well, it's not been very easy for us, you know.'

'Fortune favours the brave, and all that,' Leroy said gravely, 'but there's no stopping us now. We're going ahead.'

When Leroy had escorted Elena out of the flat to do her shopping in the small arcade adjacent to the flats, where Leroy had told Sheena that Elena worked, he was off on his travels doing the rounds of the house agents, leaving Sheena free to start her studies.

At first it was hard going. She kept thinking of Leroy and Elena, of the happiness in store for them. One day maybe she, too, would find such happiness. Again, at this moment Brad's strong features stole unbidden into her mind's eyes again, and she felt the shiver run down her spine.

'Blast the man!' she said out loud, and set to work, this time with a will, and was soon immersed in study.

Elena slipped in at lunch time, and in spite of Sheena's protest that she really didn't want a cooked lunch and could easily get herself a sandwich and a drink, Elena made them omelettes.

'Aunt Doris will be over the moon,' Elena said dreamily, as she pushed her half-eaten meal away.

'I'm too excited to eat,' she explained to Sheena.

'I thought Leroy said that your aunt didn't like him,' Sheena said.

'Oh, she does really,' Elena replied, 'but see it from her point of view. I've known him all this time, and we've had to meet in secret. I've tried to explain about his mother, but I'm sure she thinks there is some other reason. She feels that he's only playing with me. She reads all the society papers and knows what's going on, which was a good thing for me, as I wouldn't have got next week off if she hadn't been sure that Leroy would be on the trip to the outback. They gave it a lot of coverage, you know. Oddly enough, I was thinking of taking that week off anyway, my friend Carrie is having that week, and Aunt knows that too, so she isn't worried that I'll do anything stupid.'

Leroy collected Sheena at five-thirty, and on the way back he told her that he had been able to fix himself up with lodgings for the coming week from a friend who owed him a favour. 'So he's letting me borrow his flat. I've already got some brochures for Elena to look at this evening, 'he added brightly.

Sheena wondered if his mother had noticed the change in Leroy. To her he seemed a different man, full of confidence now with no sign of his previous harassed expression, and she felt that she ought to warn of this possibility.

'Well, she might have noticed,' he conceded, 'but she's so taken up with collecting all the known antidotes for whatever bug might bite me, and lecturing me on not doing this and that, that I honestly don't think she's time for anything else.

If she did begin to wonder, I'm sure she would put my enthusiasm down to the coming trip. I didn't make the mistake of pulling out too soon, either, in case someone happens to mention it to Mother. That is hardly likely, she's not too popular, you know, mainly because of her attitude, so even if someone did spot me around, the chances are they wouldn't mention it. But it's better to be safe from any possibility, so I've just said that I'll join them later. I've done if before, so no one will think it at all odd.'

At dinner that evening it was obvious that Brad had been in touch with Leroy, for he suggested that he took her out to dinner the next evening to a small restaurant famed for its cuisine.

Sheena felt that she was between the devil and the deep blue sea. She knew that he would take advantage of the fact that she was free in the evenings, but hadn't expected him to act quite so fast.

She could feel Gran's stern gaze on her as the invitation was given and could not see how she could refuse it, so she accepted. This pleased Gran and gave Brad that smug look she so detested.

The next day, Leroy collected her again and took her to Elena's flat, but this time Elena was at work by the time she got there. Sheena had to clear the small table of agents' brochures on houses for sale.

Watching her clearing the decks, Leroy said, 'Lots going, but not what we want. Still, I'm on the trail again today. I've fixed the wedding for next Friday, don't have to worry about witnesses either.

Apparently there's always staff around the place who don't mind standing in for you for a small fee. I wish it were sooner, but I suppose it does give us a few days to get sorted out,' he added cheerfully.

When he had gone, Sheena sat down at the table and arranged her notebook and manual ready to start work.

She was a dab hand at arranging other people's lives, she thought wistfully, but wasn't very clever where her own was concerned. The thought of the coming dinner with Brad that evening was uppermost in her mind. If she knew anything about him, she was sure that he would have selected the kind of place that had candlelight dinners with cosy nooks for a spot of canoodling in between the courses.

She frowned. If only he would act as other men acted and not try to dominate her so much. The fact of the matter was that he didn't seem able to keep his hands off her the minute they were alone.

Again that same old shiver ran down her back at the thought, and she was ashamed to admit that she would have felt cheated if he did behave himself!

This thought sent her back to her studies with the determination that had been lacking before, but as the day drew to a close, so her heartbeats quickened. She knew that she was in love with Brad Muldoon, for better, or as in her case, for worse, and it was something that she would have to live with.

CHAPTER NINE

SHEENA dressed for the dinner, and wore one of the two silk suits Gran had bought her. The one she chose to wear that evening was a pale yellow that suited her dark colouring, but her every action was dominated by the thought of Brad, and she quite deliberately spent extra time on her appearance. She couldn't win him, she knew, but at least she could make him remember her for a long time to come.

Brad was waiting for her in the hall as usual, and her heart did a skip and a jump as she looked at him, dressed in a dark dinner jacket and looking every inch the kind of escort women dreamed about.

This time he showed no sign of his earlier impatience. It was almost as if now that he had got his way he was content to act the perfect gentleman on a date with his chosen girlfriend. Even so, Sheena saw his swift, keen appraisal of her appearance. She knew that she was looking her best, but it was nice to have it confirmed by those enigmatic blue eyes of his.

She found that her earlier estimate of what kind of restaurant he would take her to was right on every count but one. There were candles, and there were certainly couples canoodling in the dimly lit nooks thoughtfully provided by the forward-looking proprietor. The only thing missing was Brad's failure to take advantage of the situation!

One would have thought, marvelled a bemused Sheena, that they had only just met. Here he was, asking questions about her background and her training at the hospital, and she managed to reply to these innocent-sounding questions with the right kind of deference. Yet she couldn't avoid sending him several unobtrusive glances when she thought that he wasn't looking. At least she thought they were unobtrusive, until an imp of amusement in his blue eyes told her that he had spotted them!

What was he trying to do? she wondered, Convince her of his sincerity? She all but shook her head. She wasn't that dumb! But perhaps he thought she was. It was an act, of course, to lull her into a state of complacency. Before she knew it he would revert to his he-man act, more than probably on the way home with perhaps a stop at one of the parking areas frequented by courting couples.

There was one incident after dinner that made Sheena's pulse race in anticipation, and that was when the flower girl paused at their table, and Brad chose a golden orchid for Sheena. He waved away the girl whose obvious intention was to pin it to Sheena's lapel, and performed the task himself, his strong but sure fingers lingering a moment on her throat as he secured the corsage.

It was only a small incident, but Sheena could still feel the touch of his fingers long afterwards, and it seemed to heighten the tension between them. In spite of Brad's cool outward manner, Sheena had the feeling that he was like a coiled spring that needed only a touch to make it unwind with furious speed.

There was another surprise in store for her that evening, for Brad took her back to Grasslands immediately after the dinner, with no half-way stop. She had been anticipating, with what could only be described as a shameful longing, feeling those hard lips descend on hers again, and the sensations that he, and only he, could invoke in her.

She might as well, she told herself angrily as she got ready for bed that night, have gone to dinner with Leroy! It had been about as exciting an evening! She felt let down and ill-used and didn't really calm down until she lay in bed awaiting sleep.

Just what was he up to? Her brow creased in thought, and suddenly she had it. Of course, Gran had given him a lecture on behaving himself for once, and giving Sheena no cause to turn his next invitation down! It was simple when you came to work it out, she told herself, and wondered how long he could keep it up!

She was smiling when she fell asleep. She would accept every invitation he threw her way from now on. It would be like putting him through a commando course. She didn't think he would last long enough to gain the necessary qualifications.

All she had to do, she told herself, was to annoy him, and he would throw all his good intentions out of the windows! Not that they were good intentions where she was concerned, and it was nice to think that for once she had the jump on him. No wonder he was tensed up, it must be a very long time since he had to act so much out of character, and how it must hurt!

There were two more invitations after that, one for the theatre, which Gran attended too, and one for a concert which Gran declined. On each occasion, however, Brad kept up his studiously polite behaviour and Sheena could have screamed in frustration.

As hateful as he could be, she much preferred the real Brad Muldoon, and no matter how hard she tried to provoke him, he simply smiled it off. He returned her attacks with a compliment that made her cheeks turn a rosy pink, partly in anger and partly in embarrassment.

His eyes told her that he knew very well what she was up to, and laughed at her attempts to rile him, and her eyes told him she was just aware of what he was up to, and it was hard luck because it wasn't going to work. This was all very well, but there were times when she spotted a look that told her that either way she couldn't win!

As the week drew to a close, Sheena didn't know whether to be pleased or sorry. The coming Friday was D-Day for Leroy and Elena, and she could feel the expectancy all around her in the flat as she sat at her studies. While she was very happy for them, it only served to highlight her own predicament.

She hadn't meant to fall in love with Brad, but it had happened, and whatever her hopes might have been for a reciprocal response from him, his recent attitude towards her proved his earlier point that she was wasting her time if she had any idea on ensnaring him into marriage.

By now she had reached the conclusion that he was only putting up with her company to placate Gran. There was obviously someone else in the background now that Glenda was off the scene. The very fact that he had spaced his invitations out the way he had proved to Sheena that he was only fitting her in on his free evenings.

The trouble was that Gran either couldn't or wouldn't see it. Either way, it made things worse for Sheena, for the longer she stayed, the more awkward things would become. She even contemplated following the advice she had given Leroy, and make a run for her home and freedom, but it was not that easy. There might however come a time when that was the only solution if Gran proved obstinate and took to her bed again when her going home was discussed.

On Monday she was a little dismayed to find that Brad too had the week off; the coming Wednesday party was only a little celebration partaken by the law society during that week, so Gran told her later, after Brad had said how much he was looking forward to the break.

The thought of Brad being around when Leroy called for her worried Sheena somewhat, as she could see a situation arising where Brad might suggest an outing to them. This would have to be turned down, and the thought was confirmed when she heard Leroy's car in the drive. She went out to meet him only to find that Brad had beaten her to it.

For a moment, Leroy looked like a small boy who had been caught stealing apples, and Sheena sprang to the rescue. 'Brad's got a week off, Leroy. It seems everybody's on holiday,' she added, as she got in his car.

Given the assurance that all was well, and his plot hadn't been discovered, Leroy calmed down and waved an airy hand at the car. 'Only room for one, you see,' he said, and at Brad's continuing bright blue stare, added weakly. 'Well, enjoy yourself,' and fumbling with the starter key, took off with a roar.

'Phew!' Leroy said, as they got into the main road. 'I thought my time was up then. Thought that he's found out about me and Elena. Didn't say much, did he?'

Sheena had been thinking the same thing. He had been remarkably quiet for some reason, and it wasn't a bit like him. 'Don't worry about that,' she said. 'He was a bit late getting in last night, probably has a hangover.'

'Oh, he was at that fight, I expect,' Leroy said sounding relieved. 'Went on to the early morning. Would have gone myself. It was a right ding-donger too, but our bloke held his own. As I said, I would have gone, only this outback trip started in the early hours, and Mother would have smelt a rat if I'd gone. As it was, I had to leave home around sixish armed with a case full of anti this and that,' he grinned, then his face sobered. 'You know, much as I like Brad, I don't believe he'd stand for this sort of lark.'

Sheena looked at him. 'Your marrying Elena, you mean?' she asked.

Leroy nodded. 'Not my marrying Elena, exactly, but the way we've had to do it,' he explained.

'Brad's a good fellow but he's pretty hot on family, you know, wouldn't think it was the thing at all. Look how he felt about you and that Walling feller. I've never seen him so angry. To tell the truth, I thought he'd knock the chap's head off given half a chance.'

This confirmed Sheena's thinking that Brad had put Leroy in the picture as far as she and Dean were concerned, and got him to take her out. 'It's got nothing to do with him at all!' Sheena said angrily, thinking more of her case than Leroy's. 'Can you see him doing what he was told to do?' she demanded fiercely. 'Oh, no, he pleases himself, and always will do, so he's no right to lay down the law for others. You're not having second thoughts yourself, are you, Leroy?' she demanded.

Leroy was startled at her vehemence. 'No chance,' he said firmly. 'There's never been a time when I felt happier, thanks to you. Mother will come round in time, she'll have to, I don't intend to give Elena up.

Sheena felt relieved. It would have been awful if Leroy had fallen at the post, and she ought not to have encouraged him, but happily no such event was in store, and his and Elena's dreams would come true.

The following morning the same thing happened. Brad was waiting for Leroy in the drive before Sheena got there, and again he said only a few words to Leroy before their departure.

'I'm beginning to wonder if he thinks I've got designs on you,' Leroy said to Sheena, when they were under way. 'It's not what he says, but what he doesn't say.'

'Oh, I shouldn't think so,' Sheena said. 'You know how seriously he takes his role of head of the family. I expect he thinks that he ought to show an interest.'

'Well, maybe,' Leroy replied in a tone of voice that suggested he was not entirely convinced.

However, Sheena was; she had seen enough of Brad the previous week to support this statement.

Soon it was Wednesday, and Sheena got ready for her date with Brad with a listlessness that was entirely foreign to her natural buoyancy, hating the thought of the evening ahead. If Brad had been studiously polite before, he would be even more so at this party with his colleagues. Not one of her ploys to rile him had come off. It was like hitting your head against a wall; the sooner you stopped, the better for all concerned.

The only difference this time was the fact that he had reverted to his impatience for her appearance in the hall where he waited for her.

She sensed it before she joined him, and it gave her some pleasure that perhaps at last he was beginning to crack and show his true form. Not that she had much heart for a fight now. She was too involved emotionally to get any pleasure out of it.

Sheena's thoughts were miles away, so that when Brad eventually stopped the car, she was surprised to find that they were nowhere near the government buildings, but seemed to be in what looked suspiciously like one of the parks's parking areas.

She didn't have time to ponder on this fact.

'Now you're going to answer some questons,' Brad said harshly, 'and they'd better be the right ones. I saw Leroy today emerging from a house agent's office with a pile of brochures. You were nowhere in sight. Just what is going on? Why is Leroy looking for property?'

While Sheena tried to gather her wits to give a suitable reply, Brad had been doing a little adding up of his own and got the wrong total. He caught her arm in a grip that made her wince. 'Not thinking of railroading him into a Register Office wedding, are you?' he threw at her. 'I knew you were after a rich husband, but I didn't think you wanted one that bad,' he added viciously.

'You're hurting me!' Sheena cried out as she tried to release his grip on her arm, but Brad was in no mood for niceties.

'I'll do more than hurt you,' he said savagely. 'I want the truth, and don't think I won't get it one way or another. I can always check with the Registrar.'

Sheena knew that she was beaten. If he did that it would all come out anyway, so she had better own up. 'Leroy's not in love with me,' she said. 'He's in love with somone else, a girl called Elena.'

'You mean that plump brunette from the tobacconists?' Brad asked.

Sheena stared at him. 'You knew about Elena?' she exclaimed.

'Of course I did,' Brad said bluntly. 'Most of the crowd did. Leroy's as subtle as a bull in a china-shop when it comes to hiding his feelings. Well, what

what about her?' he demanded.

Sheena took a deep breath. 'Does his mother know about her?' she asked.

He gave her a hard stare. 'I shouldn't think so, and if she did, she'd ignore her,' he replied. 'The Elenas of this world live at one end of the equator and the Leroys at the other. Does that answer your question? Now, for the last time, what's all this to do with Elena?' he asked aggressively.

'Leroy's marrying her on Friday,' Sheena said, quickly looking away from Brad's startled expression. 'That's why he was looking at the agents's brochures, to find a place of their own.'

'I see,' Brad said ominously, 'and what part exactly do you play in this little drama?'

Sheena's fingers fiddled with the safety-belt at her side, perhaps because it was a safety-belt. She would have to tell him it wasn't any use quibbling. She breathed in deeply. 'Well, I sort of suggested it,' she said.

'You what!' Brad thundered. 'What are you? Some kind of a head-shrinker? First Walling pours out his heart to you, and now Leroy. Why don't you set up an agony column in the local paper! Look, do you know what you've done? Mrs Leroy trying to be nice is bad enough, but Mrs Leroy on the warpath will be a sight to behold, I can assure you,' he prophesied grimly.

Sheena was not a bit repentant. 'He'll have to stand up to her one day,' she said angrily, 'and it might as well be sooner than later.'

'That's what you think,' Brad said. 'Ever seen a herd stampeding? Well, the dust they kick up will be nothing to the dust Mrs Leroy will raise when she hears about it. Personally, I think Leroy ought to be looking for property elsewhere, preferably somewhere in Outer Mongolia!' He gave Sheena a sideways look. 'No, you're not a head-shrinker, you're one of the patients, or ought to be.'

There was a long silence after this, until Sheena could bear it no longer and said in a small voice, 'You won't tell on them, Brad, will you?'

Brad looked at her, then shrugged. 'I guess not, as long as Leroy knows what he's getting into. He's not had much of a life so far.' he concluded quietly, then his stare became more intense. 'That explains that side of things, what exactly were you doing while Leroy was doing the rounds of the agents?'

Sheena looked down at her hands. Brad still held her arm but had relaxed his hard grip. 'Oh, I was at Elena's flat studying,' she said.

'For what?' Brad growled.

Sheena's brows rose. 'What do you think?' she replied crossly. 'I'm supposed be taking my Finals, and no matter what Gran says, I am taking them.'

Brad leaned towards her. 'Still want to be a nurse?' he asked.

'Of course I do,' Sheena returned bravely, although somehow the idea wasn't as appealing as it had been before.

'And then what?' Brad asked, his blue eyes studying her features intently.

Sheena wished that he wouldn't look at her like that. It was hard to think objectively. 'Do what I've been trained to do, of course,' she replied calmly in spite of her thudding heart.

'Well, before you go,' Brad said off-handedly, 'I'd like to consult you on a problem a friend of mine is having. You see, there's this girl who simply won't take the poor bloke seriously. He's tried every trick in the book, and it hasn't come off. What do you suggest he does?' he asked.

'Find himself another girl!' Sheena snapped out angrily. He was making fun of her now, and she simply couldn't bear it.

Brad shook his head sadly. 'No go, I'm afraid, it's her or nobody for him.'

'Well, in that case, he has my deepest sympathy,' Sheena replied tartly. 'Now, as we're not going to that party, I'd like to go back to Grasslands and start my packing.'

'I see,' Brad murmured. 'Deserting Leroy in his darkest hour, are you? It won't be you Mrs Leroy is gunning for, you know, it will be Elena.'

'I'm not——' began Sheena, then gave it up. What was the use? She was just a figure of fun to him, and always would be. However, he was right in one thing, she couldn't leave until the deed was done, but very soon afterwards, she promised herself, she would.

Sheena decided to say nothing to Gran about her decision to leave. She was a coward and knew it, but this time she meant it, and wasn't going to give her any other option but to give in.

If Gran had wondered why they were back from the party so early—although she had gone to bed by the time they got back, she would have relied upon Milly to keep her up to date with events—she would have assumed, quite wrongly this time, that they had quarrelled again.

On the Thurday morning, Leroy picked her up at the usual time, although Sheena had suggested that perhaps he might have more to see to than to bother with conveying her to Elena's flat, but he had been adamant on this. Where would they be now, but for her? The least they could do was help her in her studies. He also told her that she was quite welcome to use the flat while they were away on their honeymoon right after the ceremony.

So Thursday was no exception to the rule, and a happy Leroy was slightly surprised to find no sign of Brad when he arrived in the drive.

For Sheena's part, she knew only relief which later turned to scorn. Who was chicken now? she thought. It was obvious that Brad hadn't trusted himself not to say something that would give the game away. He had given his word, and meant to abide by it.

'We've settled on a place on the outskirts,' Leroy said. 'and we're prepared for any incursion into our privacy.' His face sobered for a moment. 'I wish it could have been different, but there you are.' He looked at the thoughtful Sheena. 'You're very quiet this morning,' he said.

Sheena had been thinking of Brad's remarks on where he would advise them to settle, but of course she could not tell Leroy this, not at this stage of the proceedings. She had to say something. 'It's all this studying, Leroy,' she replied. 'Not that I mind, it will stand me in good stead when I get back.'

This satisfied Leroy, who then suddenly remembered something he had to ask her. 'Look, do you mind if we use the flat this afternoon? We've lots of loose ends to tie up and it would be more convenient if we used Elena's place to sort them out.'

Sheena hastily assured him that of course she didn't mind, they could use it that morning if they liked. He could drop her somewhere in the city, but Leroy told her that Elena was out for the morning having a hairdo, and that he would pick her up around twelve-thirty.

She got back to Grassland around one o'clock, to find Brad and Gran finishing their lunch, and in spite of her protests that she wasn't a bit hungry she had to wait until Milly fixed her a salad.

By the time she had finished it was close on two, and she knew that she would have to go and join Brad and Gran in the lounge. It would look odd if she didn't, but she certainly did not fancy a cosy chat with either Gran or Brad. It did occur to her that Brad might take it into his head to warn Gran of her coming departure, and he could start a lot of trouble for her. Not that he cared one way or the other. As usual it was Gran he was looking out for.

She had only just entered the lounge and was about to sit down when Milly appeared at the door. 'There's a Mrs Leroy to see Miss Fairburn,' she announced.

Gran's first reaction was one of annoyance. 'What does she want?' she asked, then addressing Milly, said, 'Put her in the study, Milly, we'll never get rid of her if she comes in here.'

Sheena's eyes went straight to Brad who met her

panic-stricken look with raised brows. 'Hadn't you better see what she wants?' he said, galvanising her into action, and escorting her to the door he murmured *sotto voce*, 'and fasten your seat-belt!'

Just the kind of advice she needed, she thought angrily, as she made her way to the study, wondering what on earth she could say to the woman if she had uncovered the plot.

The woman who rose to meet her as she walked into the room was of vast proportions, calling to mind Brad's words about the amount of dust she would kick up when roused. As this was not the time to recall such incidentals, Sheena swallowed and forced herself to walk forward and shake the plump well ringed hand extended towards her, only just recovering her aplomb to realise that she actually was holding out her hand to her.

'We haven't had the pleasure of meeting, Miss Fairburn,' she said in a strident voice which Sheena was sure could be heard by Gran and Brad behind two doors down the passage. She hoped that they couldn't hear the rest of the conversation, although Mrs Leroy seemed friendly enough.

'I know that you must be missing my Leroy,' she went on, favouring Sheena with a sickly coy look. 'So I rather wondered if you'd care to take tea with me this afternoon.'

Sheena was at a loss to reply to what was obviously a royal command. She had no wish to sit in that room of purple splendour exchanging banalities with a woman who was in for an awful shock in the very near future. 'Well, I——'

This was as far as she got, for at this point

the door opened and Brad walked in. 'Oh,' he exclaimed, in a voice meant to convey that he had no idea that Sheena had company, 'Mrs Leroy! How are you?'

Sheena could not help but admire the way Brad charmed the woman, who turned positively gushy in his presence and started to explain the reason for her visit, ending with her invitation to Sheena to join her for tea that afternoon.

'Now that's a pity,' Brad said, 'but we were just on our way out to a prior engagement. I'm sure Sheena appreciates your invitation. Some other time, perhaps?' Like a magician he conjured her away to the front door before she could begin to suggest another date.

'Well?' Gran said impatiently. 'What did she want? I warned Sheena about that woman. Give her an inch and she'll take a yard.'

Brad smiled at her. 'Don't worry, Gran. She won't be calling again,' he assured her.

'I wish I could be sure of that,' Gran muttered, 'and you haven't told me what she wanted.'

'Sheena's company for tea,' Bran replied with a wicked smile. 'I only just saved her from having to accept the offer, and for that she owes me.' He gave Sheena a meaningful glance.

'I would have thought of something,' Sheena said, now past the grateful stage for Brad's help, 'but you barged in just as I was working something out.'

'Now that would have been a grave mistake,' Brad said airily. 'A woman like Mrs Leroy would have had you wrapped up and delivered before you could draw breath.'

'I thought that's how it would be,' Gran said. 'She's got her eye on you, Sheena, for that boy of hers. She's been trying to off-load him for years now. He must be all of thirty. I advise you to keep your distance from now on,' she warned her. 'I know you like him, but now that you've met his mother I'm sure you appreciate my warnings.'

'I said not to worry, Gran,' Brad said, his eyes asssuring her of this fact.

Gran stared at him, then acknowledged the look he sent her, and said meekly, 'Very well.' She took up her crochet again without another word.

Sheena half expected Brad to seek some kind of compensation for his timely intervention, but to her surprise he failed to claim her company that evening, which was one way she had thought he would wangle it. Instead, he said something about being late for an appointment, and left shortly afterwards.

Just for once, Sheena found herself alone during the latter part of the evening after Gran had gone to bed. She took the opportunity of doing some packing, and was careful to place her suitcase in the wardrobe away from Milly's keen glance afterwards, so that she wouldn't have so much to do when the time came.

She was grateful that Brad had not yet told Gran that she was going home. He had his reasons, no doubt, she thought. If Gran didn't know, she couldn't stop her, could she? She was sure that that would be his reasoning.

Only one more day, she told herself, just before she went to sleep, and there would be no more hassle, no more trying to avoid awkward situations—no more Brad Muldoon!

CHAPTER TEN

FRIDAY was D-Day not only for Leroy and Elena, it was D-Day for Sheena too.

She would have to go to the flat in the morning as usual, for she had promised to help Elena get ready for her wedding, but as soon as Elena had gone, she was to be off herself.

She had it all worked out. She would come back to Grasslands and tell Gran that she wanted to go home, indeed she was going home, and hoped that she understood.

This was as far as she always got before her courage failed her, but somehow she had to go through with it. She was unhappy, and Gran must be made to see that, and surely . . . ?

Friday dawned bright and beautiful for a wedding day, but no such happiness could be found in Sheena's heart.

She had tried to look ahead, to start planning what she would do once she got back to Victoria. First see the Matron and arrange to start back at work, and hope that she would agree to her taking her Finals with the rest of the students. She had studied most of the subjects likely to come up at the tests, and if she didn't pass, well, there was always next year.

This thought sent her plunging down into the depths again, and it was all she could do to give back

Brad's cheerful 'Good morning' as she met him on the way to the dining-room. His comment of, 'Cheer up, it might never happen,' made her flash him a suspicious look, until he added, 'whatever it is you're worried about.'

As long as he didn't intend to put a spoke in Leroy's plans, he could think what he liked, Sheena thought dourly as they joined Gran at the table.

'Are you off with that Leroy this morning?' Gran demanded.

Sheena glanced at her. 'Last day, Gran. I couldn't very well put him off at the last moment, could I?' She made a point of not looking at Brad.

Leroy arrived a little earlier that morning, which was not surprising as this was his big day, and Sheena was annoyed to find that Brad was deep in conversation with him by the time she joined him. If he said anything to put him off, she would hate him for the rest of her life, she thought angrily, and glared at him.

Whatever it was, it had not affected Leroy's buoyant spirits, she noticed, and gave an inward sight of relief.

'I won't come in this time, Sheena,' he said, 'you know the old saying about the groom not seeing the bride and all that.'

Sheena nodded. She knew that she ought to tell him that she would not be taking their offer of the use of the flat while they were away, that she herself would be going home, but she couldn't bring herself to mention it. She would leave a note for them thanking them for the help they had given her in her studies, and wish them every happiness in the future.

Just before they reached the flat, Leroy said, 'You know, Sheena, I wish you could have been one of our witnesses, and Brad, too, of course, but Elena and I felt it wasn't fair to get you embroiled in the actual deed. It's better if no one else is involved.'

Sheena had stopped listening when he mentioned Brad, and she looked at him. 'Brad?' she queried.

Leroy pulled up in the courtyard of the flats. 'Blast!' he said. 'I wasn't supposed to let you know that. He told me that he'd got it out of you, but fair dos, he's not splitting on us. Look, Sheena, Brad's OK. I know you don't get on with him, but you might give it a try some time, and not jump down his throat when he calls to collect you this morning.'

Sheena stared at him. 'He's collecting me?' she exclaimed. 'Here, at Elena's flat? Whatever for?'

Leroy kicked the front tyre of his car savagely. 'Something else I shouldn't have mentioned,' he said ruefully. 'It's only a bit of fun on his part. Said something about asking your advice on a problem with a friend, said you owed him a favour anyway.'

Sheena's brow darkened. 'That was what he said, was it?' she queried with a gleam in her eyes as she got out of the car.

Leroy saw her to the door of the flat. 'Well, something like that,' he said, 'I think he was pretty impressed by the way you sorted me and Elena out, you know,' he added.

'Goodbye, Leroy!' Sheena said, with more emphasis than was necessary, and caused him to give her an uncertain look that made her relent. 'Well, thanks for warning me,' she said, 'and have a lovely day.'

Once she had entered the flat, there was not much time to dwell on her own problems as Elena was in a state of nerves, and as soon as she saw Sheena, she rushed at her. 'Sheena! Am I doing the right thing?' she appealed to her, and so it went on for most of the morning. Elena was torn between her wish to marry Leroy and the way they had to do it, but eventually Sheena calmed her down, and by the time she was dressed in a wine velvet suit and matching blouse she was ready for the fray.

In the midst of all this, Sheena had not forgotten Leroy's warning about Brad calling for her. Not that Leroy had looked upon it as a warning, but to Sheena's way of thinking it quite definitely was.

She had a pretty good idea what he had in mind. He knew that she was determined to go home, and this was probably the last chance that he would get at cornering her.

She wouldn't put anything past him. His ego had been somewhat dented, and someone had to pay for that. She didn't need two guesses as to who it would be!

This thought sent her searching for a telephone directory, and looking up the number of the coach station to enquire about departures to Victoria. Trains would be quicker, but Sheena hadn't enough money to pay for the fare. As it was she wouldn't be able to go the whole way, but near enough to get Mary to send Don to collect her without making it too far a journey.

She found that she had to be at the coach station at two p.m. if she wanted to be sure of getting a ticket, and by hook or by crook that was what she would do.

She then scribbled a note to Elena and Leroy, and rang for a taxi to collect her. Snatching up all her books she had to force herself to wait patiently for the taxi's arrival. There ought to be enough time, for she had twenty minutes in hand. Usually Leroy collected her at twelve-thirty, and he would have told Brad this, but you could never tell with that man, he might just decide to work out what time Elena would have left the flat and go on from there.

To her vast relief she was well away from the flat within five minutes of her call for a taxi and on the way to Grasslands. She rehearsed in her mind what she would say to Gran. It was now or never, and she couldn't afford to let sentiment get in her way. She had the rest of her life ahead of her, and hopefully some chance of happiness.

Shortly before twelve-thirty, Sheena was back at Grasslands and went in search of Gran, who this time was on the patio taking in the warm rays of the sun.

Without giving herself time to have second thoughts, she plunged in at the deep end, ending with, 'I've made my mind up, Gran. It's time I got on with my life. I'm not a lounge-lizard, and honestly, I'd be much happier back at work, so I'll be off after lunch.'

Gran looked at her. 'Does Brad know?' she asked.

Sheena blinked. She had expected a show of indignation from Gran, and the inevitable argument, but here she was calmly asking if Brad knew that she was going. 'Yes, he knows,' she replied. 'He was the first one I told, as a matter of fact,' she added for good measure.

Gran nodded thoughtfully. 'Well, I'm sorry, of course. I shall miss you, Sheena, but as I said before, you can't run others' lives for them. The main thing is for you to be happy, and I'm sure you know what you're doing. You will keep your promise to come and see me in your vacation period, won't you?' she said.

A slightly bemused Sheena agreed that of course she would keep her promise, and quickly excused herself on the grounds that she had some last-minute packing to do before lunch.

Sheena made her way to her room in an utterly confused state. To think how much she had worried over telling Gran she was going, and how unnecessary it had been.

Back in her room she collected her things and pushed them willy-nilly into her suitcase, hesitating over the things her Gran had bought her. She decided to leave them. She told herself that this would be a sign to Gran that she did mean to come back.

That done, she sat on the bed and tried to collect her senses. One thing stood out a mile, and that was that Gran had expected this to happen. She had not been at all surprised, but had taken it with a calm composure that was not at all in keeping with her earlier outlook.

Sheena sighed deeply. There could be only one reason. Brad had at last got through to her, made her face up to the simple fact that her pipe-dream was a pipe-dream, and had no place in reality.

Sheena gave an impatient shrug and got off the bed. It certainly had taken her long enough to see it,

MULDOON TERRITORY   173

and it must have taken a pretty strong argument
from Brad to accomplish it.

Perhaps he had told her that he had met the one
and only girl, and this time she had all the right
connections that would fit in with Gran's idea of the
kind of wife for him.

She swallowed on this thought, then whispered
fiercely, 'It's no business of mine who he chooses!'

They had just begun lunch when Brad stormed in.
That was the only way to describe his entrance into
the dining-room. With a set jaw and blazing eyes, he
ground out to Sheena. 'Left early, didn't you? I told
Leroy I'd pick you up.'

Sheena looked at him, and widened her eyes inno-
cently. 'Leroy said nothing about that,' she said.

For a moment, it looked as if he might have
argued this fact, then gave her a steely eye as he sat
down at the table. 'Knowing Leroy, I would have
thought he might have mentioned it,' he added
meaningly.

'Well, he didn't,' Sheena lied valiantly, thinking
how right she had been to cut and run for it. He had
intended to have one last go at her before her
imminent departure.

'If Sheena didn't know that you were calling for
her, I don't see why you're so angry, Brad,' Gran
said quietly. 'Do let's have some peace with our
lunch. By the way, did you know that——'

At this point the telephone extension in the
dining-room rang, and with a sigh Brad got up to
answer it, to the vast relief of Sheena. She had been
certain that Gran had been about to tell him of her
departure directly after lunch, and the last thing she

wanted was to have him convey her to the coach station, no doubt wishing her luck with her quest for a rich husband, and how sorry he was that he hadn't been able to oblige!

'Look, can't you find someone else?' Brad was demanding exasperatedly. 'I know I said I'd help out, but this is damned short notice.' There was a silence, then he said. 'Well, OK. See you,' and slamming the receiver down, he walked to the door. 'They're one short for the Canberra eight, Wally Cook's gone down with some sort of flu bug, and they're due for the off in an hour's time.' He sent a rueful glance at Milly who had just appeared with a piled-up plate. 'Just as well I hadn't got that down me,' he said. 'Save it for later, Milly.' With a look that took in Gran and Sheena, lingering longer on Sheena, he said, 'See you,' and was off.

Gran looked annoyed, but Sheena felt that she had been given a reprieve and meant to take full advantage of it.

'Why did they have to call Brad,' Gran complained. 'They've a big membership, and surely they could have come up with someone else—but not as good as Brad, I suppose.' Milly, taking their plates away, nodded in complete agreement with this sentiment. 'Well, you'll have to wait until tomorrow, now, Sheena,' Gran said firmly, 'You can't go before Brad gets back.'

Sheena had to do some quick thinking. She had already made arrangements with the taxi driver who had brought her back to Grasslands to pick her up at one forty-five, which gave her ample time to get to the coach station. 'Oh, but I must go today, Gran,

I've told Mary to expect me,' she said, hoping to be forgiven for yet another white lie. The situation seemed to warrant such measures.

. For a minute it looked as if Gran was about to suggest that she rang Mary and told her of the change of plan, then suddenly she gave in, and nodded. 'Very well,' she said quietly, adding softly, 'perhaps it's as well.'

For a horrible moment, Sheena wondered whether Gran knew more than she should have done. The fact that she was fond of Brad would have made her hold her tongue, but how very disappointed in him she must have been if she had come upon the truth. It was all Sheena could do not to burst out with something on the lines of when all was said and done Brad was a man, and his instincts, like all other men, were purely predatory when it came to young women.

She could also have reminded her that she could hardly blame him for taking advantage of the situation that she herself had thrown at him. All this went through her head, but she could not bring herself actually to voice her thoughts. For one thing, she might do more harm than good if her guess was wrong, and Gran had no inkling of Brad's real intentions where she was concerned.

A quick glance at the dining-room clock told her that she had only five minutes to go upstairs and get her case down before the taxi called. She excused herself and went to collect it.

At last she was in the taxi complete with her case, and heading for the coach station, leaving Gran and Milly waving farewell on the doorstep. She felt for some illogical reason that she had let everyone down, and wanted to shout out that it wasn't her fault Brad Muldoon didn't fancy being shackled to her for life! She just wasn't good enough for him, and that was that!

As the taxi neared the end of the drive, she caught a glimpse of Stanley waving a garden fork at her, and this depressed her even further. No doubt Milly had kept him up to date with events as she had her employer.

Sheena sat back and made an effort to concentrate on anything but the fact that she was leaving Grasslands. She had already checked her monetary state, and would have to remember to leave enough to telephone Mary when she had got as far as she could.

It was odd, she mused, that Gran hadn't thought to enquire how she was travelling. Perhaps she had thought that she had enough for the train fare? Although this was not like her, and Sheena surmised that disappointment had dulled normal thoughtfulness where she was concerned.

Sheena shrugged. There she went again! She was free, and it was the future she had to look out for now. As for her promise to visit Gran as soon as she had some leave due, well, she only hoped that there would be a decent lapse of time before she kept that promise.

It was possible, of course, that once back in her own environment she would look back on her visit to Canberra as part of a growing-up exercise. She was an entirely different person from the girl who had arrived at Canberra station, hot and bothered with the long journey, and at odds with everything to do with the Muldoon clan.

Not that Brad's welcome did anything to change that outlook, she thought, and winced at the memory. Well, nothing really had changed in that respect. She was still the poor relation, good enough to play with, but the rules were his, and woe betide her if she stepped out of line. How many times had he warned her that she was out of her league? That she didn't belong, and never would.

The more she thought about the past, the better she felt about everything. No matter what, she still had her pride. There would be lots of Brad Muldoons around, the type who took what they wanted and never gave a thought to others. Thank goodness she had had the sense to get out while the going was good.

There were plenty of good men about like Mary's Don, too, she told herself, and if she were fortunate she would meet such a man. Something inside her rebelled at this point. No, she wouldn't, it whispered fiercely. If she couldn't have Brad, she didn't want anyone. They could all emigrate as far as she was concerned, and it was just her bad luck that the one and only man for her was beyond her reach.

The coach station was reached in good time, and Sheena collected her ticket. A glance at the milling crowds around her as she queued for her ticket, and she could see why the booking clerk had warned her to be in good time to book her seat.

She had managed to get as near as forty miles from home, and as she had hoped this was a reasonable journey for Don to make to pick her up.

She would, perhaps, have to wait a while for his appearance. It all depended when he finished work.

At two-thirty they were allowed to board the bus, and Sheena wished that she had been able to afford to buy one or two paperbacks to read, or even a newspaper, but she had cut things pretty fine as it was. She would have to leave enough to buy a drink at one of the stops on the way, and enough for the phone call to Mary.

Time hung while she waited for the bus to start on the journey. It was full, and all around her were the rustlings of paper bags when passengers consumed late lunches, and the softer rustling of papers being read and refolded. If she were fortunate, someone might offer her one during the course of the journey, she thought, and settled down, trying to take refuge in a doze.

A commotion roused her about ten minutes before the bus was due to start. The first thought that came into her mind was that someone was trying to board without a ticket, although there was no hope of whoever it was getting a seat. There were already children sitting on their parents' laps.

Whatever it was, it was certainly providing entertainment for the passengers, most of them leaning towards the windows to get a better look at proceedings.

Sheena had her own troubles to worry about, and leaned back and closed her eyes. Even had she wanted to watch what was going on, her view was obscured by a large lady who occupied the window seat, who had been in the process of devouring a large, gooey hamburger liberally sprinkled with ketchup.

Her peace was suddenly shattered by a voice she knew only too well. 'There she is!' She opened her eyes to find an irate Brad pointing an accusing finger at her.

Her bemused mind only had time to take in the fact that he wore the bright blue blazer of the famous rowing club, which seemed to match the colour of his eyes. Before she realised his intention he had her by the arm and was dragging her from her seat.

'Strewth, mate,' argued the flustered driver. 'You can't do that!'

'Oh, can't I?' Brad growled. 'Just watch me!' With one hand gripping Sheena's arm preventing her from regaining her seat, he turned to the driver. 'What would you do, mate, if your woman walked out on you?' he demanded, and said to Sheena, 'You're coming home.'

An outraged Sheena shouted back, 'I'm not coming home. I'm *going* home.' She glanced back to judge how far away she was from her seat, ready to make a swift dive back. She was somewhat diverted by the sight of red globules of ketchup slowly but surely dripping on to the seat, completely ignored by her erstwhile travelling companion who was gazing in open-mouthed fascination at the preceedings.

'Now look here,' the driver began uncertainly.

'No,' Brad said harshly, 'you look at it from my point of view. It's not only me, there's three kids back there crying their eyes out.'

There were rustlings among the crowd, and many 'ohs' and 'ahs' and a few 'shames'.

The driver sent Sheena an indignant look and

stood aside abruptly. 'Help yourself, mate,' he said to Brad, who needed no second bidding, but whisked an utterly confounded Sheena off the bus, amid murmurs of, 'They're all the same these days, just want a good time.'

Brad kept a vice-like grip on her arm as the bus doors closed and the driver climbed into his seat, then he hustled her towards his car parked outside the station, and all but pushed her in.

It was only then that Sheena caught her breath as she watched the bus disappear into the distance. 'My luggage is on that bus!' she said furiously. 'How dare you tell such lies? Three children!' she spluttered.

'I didn't say they were yours, did I?' Brad said smoothly. 'As for your luggage, I'll replace whatever you need. We can pick that up later.'

This smooth assumption made Sheena want to scream. He had an answer for everything except one. 'Do you realise that some of the people on that bus might one day be patients of mine?' she ground out. 'That wouldn't have occurred to you, would it? Not as long as you get your way.'

'It wouldn't have occurred to me simply because you're——' he broke off, and stared in the car mirror. 'This looks like an emergency,' he said, and looked at Sheena. 'Your chickens have come home to roost,' he commented, before stepping out of the car, and opening the door of the back seats then said, 'In here.'

An amazed Sheena watched as first a tearful Elena tumbled into the car, followed by a hunted-looking Leroy.

'Keep down,' Brad ordered, keeping his eye on his wing mirror. 'Your mother's just got out of a taxi.'

Neither Leroy nor Elena needed any second bidding and crouched down on the floor of the car as Brad pressed the starter and glided smoothly off, passing the determined march of Mrs Leroy, too intent on her quarry to bother to look at the passing cars.

'It's all right, you can get up now,' Brad said as the car swept into the stream of the city traffic. 'Mission accomplished?' he asked, meeting Leroy's eyes in the front mirror.

Leroy started, then gathered his wits about him, and nodded gloomily. 'But that's as far as we got,' he said, 'we were on our way out when I spotted Mother coming in, and we dived for the back entrance, but of course she saw us. As luck would have it we caught a passing taxi, there was no hope of picking up my car. That blighter Dawson stood on guard beside it, Mother's orders of course.'

Sheena forgot her own troubles for a moment and asked, 'But how?'

Leroy caught Elena's hand. 'Because I haven't the brains I was born with,' he replied angrily. 'Things had gone too smoothly, I suppose, but no one but a fool would have left their car right on the forecourt of the Registrar's office, which is what I did. The second thing I overlooked was the fact that Dawson has Friday off. He must have spotted the car on his way to the library. Great reader, is Dawson. Anyway, he must have stopped to check up if it was my car, and then rung mother. It's just the sort of thing he would do. He knew damn well I was supposed to be somewhere in the outback.'

'So where to now?' Brad asked. 'Got any plans?'

Leroy sighed. 'Not really. All I could think of was to get to the bus station and jump on one of those roving tours; they leave pretty frequently. A train would have taken too long, getting the tickets and everything. You pay as you enter on those buses, but we need that car, all our luggage is in it.'

It wasn't a good day for luggage, Sheena thought idly; hers was heading for Victoria right now.

'Well, in that case, we'll have to think of something that will draw that watchdog off. Got it!' exclaimed Brad. 'I happen to know one of the staff there, shout out when anyone sees a call box,' he ordered.

A call box was found conveniently near the Registrar's office, and Brad managed to park well back from the forecourt but in a position that gave them full view of the parking area. 'Look at him,' Leroy said angrily, as all eyes were centred on the lounging figure of Dawson leaning against the car doors. 'I wondered that he doesn't try and climb in,' he added bitterly.

Brad was gone only a few minutes, and then rejoined them. 'Now we wait,' he said, 'I've sent a message to Dawson, purporting to come from your mother, Leroy, asking him to join her at the coach station. I hope it works.'

'Oh, it'll work all right,' Leroy said happily. 'No one argues with Mother.'

Sure enough, a minute later someone approached Dawson and had a few words with him, and he immediately left his post and walked to an old station wagon parked further along the line. Shortly afterwards passed them on his way to join his employer.

A jubilant Leroy clutched Brad's hand, 'I can't thank you enough——' he began.

'I presume you have the car keys?' Brad interrupted quickly. 'I suggest you get cracking.'

Leroy needed no second prompting, and, grabbing the silent Elena's hand, got out of the car, patting his trouser pocket. 'That's one thing I did remember to do,' he said, before giving them a final wave and hurrying Elena over to the car.

A triumphant toot of the horn as they swept away was their last communication.

For a second Brad and Sheena were silent, both thinking of Leroy and Elena, then a flurry at the door of the Registrar's caught their attention. A young couple stood in the doorway surrounded by friends and relations congratulating them, then at the instigation of a friend with a camera they shyly kissed, amid laughter.

'Now that's what I call a sensible arrangement,' Brad said, then looked at Sheena. 'What's it to be?' he growled. 'That, or a lot of hoo-hah?'

Sheena stared at him. 'Brad Muldoon! Are you asking me to marry you?' she asked indignantly.

'I should have thought that even you would have cottoned on to that. If you hadn't been in such an all-fired hurry to leave that flat, we'd have got it all cut and dried by now,' he added accusingly.

'And you thought that all you had to do was to ask me?' Sheena enquired angrily. 'Pretty sure of yourself, weren't you?'

Brad looked at her. 'Let's put it this way,' he said smoothly. 'I'm your man, and you know it, in spite of that nasty habit you have of contradicting everything I say. I can tell you one thing, we wouldn't have left that flat until I'd made you see it!'

'That's precisely why I did leave early,' Sheena said coldly. 'I thought that was what you had in mind.'

'So you did know I was picking you up!' Brad exclaimed angrily. 'And you couldn't be bothered to let me say my piece!'

Sheena bristled. 'What did you expect?' she demanded indignantly. 'I'm not a fool; I'd had one dubious offer from you the last time you tried a bit of persuasion on me.'

Brad had the grace to look rueful, and ran a hand through his hair. 'Well, I guess I asked for that,' he said, 'but that was before I realised why it was that I got so damned angry at you for no apparent reason. I took one look at you, and nothing seemed the same again. I thought it was because you and Gran had hatched up a plot to trap me into marriage, and I wasn't going to be railroaded on those terms.'

Sheena stayed silent. What he had said was true. She had thought the same herself.

'It was only when you let yourself go, and let me really kiss you, that I realised what the trouble with me was. I had to admit that any man who wanted you would have to get past me first, and no way was that going to happen.' He caught her hand. 'The next part was harder, getting you to feel the

the same way as I did. There were times when I
thought you did, but on the other hand I couldn't be
sure. Like what happened over my calling for you at
the flat. I was almost certain that you did know I was
coming, and the fact that you chose to walk out on
me gave me a few bad moments. It was only when
you said that you didn't know that I felt I still had a
chance with you.'

There were tears in Sheena's eyes as she said
softly, 'There was another reason that you haven't
taken into consideration,' she said softly. 'I ran
because I had to. I couldn't trust myself to go on
saying no to you, no matter what you wanted of me.'

Brad caught her shoulders and made her look at
him, his blue eyes searching hers, then with a shout
of triumph he pulled her towards him, but the
confines of the car somewhat restricted the embrace.
'Let's get out of here,' he said, 'and find somewhere
where we can really talk.'

Sheena didn't think that it was talking he had in
mind, but she had to agree that the main street of a
busy city was not exactly ideal for their purpose.

They stopped in the same park that Leroy had
taken her to for their tête-à-tête on his problems.
How different it was for her now, she thought, with
a heart bursting with happiness. Her hand caught
Brad's as they walked down a shaded walkway, and
the minute they found a secluded bower he took her
into his arms.

A long time afterwards, they drifted back to the
car, and Brad's first remark about putting Gran out
of her misery made Sheena sit up and reluctantly
come down from cloud nine. 'We'll stay with Gran,

won't we, Brad?' she asked anxiously.

'It will be Gran who will be staying with us,' Brad said with a grin. 'In the midst of all this excitement I haven't had time to tell you that we're moving back into farming. It was an aim of mine I've had for years, and Gran knows it. We still have a dairy farm south of Sydney. Our manager is retiring at the end of this year, which gives me ample time to pick up the reins before he goes.' He looked at Sheena. 'We'll have no time for parties, and precious little time for socialising, my love, but like Gran, I don't think that will worry you.'

Sheena's answer was in her eyes, and Brad was half inclined to take her for another walk. However, he gave a regretful sigh, and started the engine. 'Gran,' he said firmly.

'Took your time,' Gran grumbled, when they walked into the lounge at Grasslands, but her eyes were anxious as they went from Sheena to Brad.

'Sorry, Gran,' Brad said with a twinkle in his eye, and pulled Sheena towards him,' but it was worth it. Sheena's agreed to become a farmer's wife.'

'About time, too,' was Gran's only comment, but her eyes were shining with pleasure at the news. 'Not such an old duffer, after all, am I?' She appealed to no one in particular. 'Now I suppose we shall have to arrange the wedding date.'

'Hold on there,' Brad said quickly. 'We've—er—sort of agreed to follow Leroy's example and plump for a special licence.'

Gran stared at him. 'Leroy?' she queried.

Brad and Sheena looked at each other. 'I suppose we'd better come clean,' Sheena said with a smile, and brought Gran up to date with recent events.

'You mean to say that all the time you were supposed to be going out with Leroy he was seeing this other woman?' Gran demanded.

Sheena nodded. 'Well, he had been seeing this other woman, as you put it, for three years, but Elena wouldn't have been good enough for his mother, so he had to keep their meetings secret,' she broke off here.

Brad, however, wasn't going to let her off scot-free. 'And——?' he added suggestively.

Sheena gave him a mock stern look. 'Well, I sort of pushed him into making his mind up. He was terribly unhappy, Gran, and I didn't think it was fair.'

Gran looked at Sheena, then burst out chuckling. 'Good for you,' she said. 'That woman's nothing to be all that proud of. They're tradesfolk themselves. She was a draper's daughter, if I remember rightly,' she added musingly, then she said to Brad, 'So you're going for a special licence, are you?'

Brad gave Sheena a hug. 'I gave her the choice, Gran, but she can still change her mind. Come to think of it, I think that was one question she didn't answer.'

Sheena smiled. 'He just said did I want a lot of hoo-hah, or a sensible arrangement, Gran. As I don't like a lot of fuss, I agree with Brad's choice.'

Gran gave her a hard look. 'Are you sure, Sheena?' she asked. 'There's only one wedding day, you know.'

'That's what's worrying me,' Brad said wickedly. 'Just how long would a grand wedding take to arrange? Say two to three months? Can you see us lasting that long without at least two bust-ups? Oh, no. I'm not giving her the chance of walking out on me again. Once I've got that ring on her finger, I've got her for keeps.'

Gran left them looking into each other's eyes, saying something about how much Sheena would love the old homestead where Sheena's mother's father was born, and Brad's great-aunt was born, and that after dinner that evening she would get out the album and show her. Though she knew that not one word was heard by either of them!